A Tom Marlowe Adventure

Redwulf's Curse

C H R I S   P R I E S T L E Y

CORGI BOOKS

REDWULF'S CURSE
A CORGI BOOK 978 0 552 55483 1

First published in Great Britain by Doubleday,
an imprint of Random House Children's Publishers UK

Doubleday edition published 2005
Corgi edition published 2006

5 7 9 10 8 6

Set in Sabon MT by
Falcon Oast Graphic Art Ltd.

Corgi Books are published by Random House Children's Publishers UK
61–63 Uxbridge Road, London W5 5SA,
a division of The Random House Group Ltd,
in Australia by Random House Australia (Pty) Ltd,
20 Alfred Street, Milsons Point, Sydney, NSW 2061, Australia,
in New Zealand by Random House New Zealand Ltd,
18 Poland Road, Glenfield, Auckland 10, New Zealand,
and in South Africa by Random House (Pty) Ltd,
Isle of Houghton, Corner Boundary Road & Carse O'Gowrie,
Houghton 2198, South Africa

THE RANDOM HOUSE GROUP Limited Reg. No. 954009
www.randomhousechildrens.co.uk

A CIP catalogue record for this book is available from the British Library.

The Random House Group Limited supports The Forest Stewardship
Council® (FSC®), the leading international forest-certification organisation.
Our books carrying the FSC label are printed on FSC®-certified paper.
FSC is the only forest-certification scheme supported by the leading
environmental organisations, including Greenpeace. Our
paper procurement policy can be found at
www.randomhouse.co.uk/environment

Printed and bound in Great Britain by Clays Ltd, St Ives plc

For the staff and children of
Snettisham Primary School

1

A Letter from Norfolk

Tom Marlowe flexed his fingers one by one and then squeezed the sword hilt tightly, chewing nervously on the inside of his bottom lip. A handcart clattered by in the alley beyond the courtyard wall and Tom took half a pace forward.

Dr Harker lunged, the tip of his sword jabbing straight at Tom's heart. Tom parried the thrust clumsily, only just sidestepping the attack, before stumbling on a loose cobble and almost falling over.

Before Tom could ready himself, Dr Harker swung his sword and Tom heard the whistle of the blade as it sliced the air between them. Again Dr Harker's sword whistled by, but this time Tom raised his own to meet it and the blades crashed together.

Dr Harker pushed into Tom so that the blades were crossed in front of their faces, their swords locked hilt to hilt. Tom saw a half smile flicker across Dr Harker's face and then the doctor gave one great shove and Tom sailed backwards, landing on his backside on a heap of sacks.

Tom struggled to get to his feet, but no sooner had he begun to raise himself up than he saw Dr Harker standing over him, the tip of his sword at Tom's throat. Tom refused to concede defeat and tried to stand. Dr Harker cocked his head on one side and raised an eyebrow. Tom sighed and dropped his sword onto the cobbles.

'Come on, Tom,' said Dr Harker, holding out a hand. 'Do not be so hard on yourself. You are coming along remarkably well.'

Tom muttered under his breath. 'I can't see that I will ever get the hang of this,' he said.

'Nonsense, Tom,' said the doctor, helping his assistant to his feet. 'I do have rather a head start on you. And at least these swords are only wooden ones.'

Tom smiled despite himself. He straightened himself up, touched swords with Dr Harker and readied himself for another bout, determined to give his all this time.

Doctor Harker traced a small circle in the air with the tip of his sword. Tom decided to attack while he still had the element of surprise and lunged forward, but as quickly as he attacked, Dr Harker dodged the thrust, stepping inside it, parrying Tom's sword arm with his free hand and grabbing his sleeve. The tip of the doctor's sword was now once again at Tom's throat. Tom was forced to simply smile and shake his head in admiration.

'You nearly had me there, Tom,' said Dr Harker. 'You are improving.'

'Not quickly enough, sir,' Tom replied.

'Come now, Tom,' said the doctor. 'Let me show you what I did there.' And the doctor took Tom through the previous movement. 'These dreadful Italian fencing masters wave their free hand about as if they are waving to their tailor across the street. They have clearly never fought for their lives.' Tom lunged and Dr Harker parried, showing him how to throw his opponent off balance. 'You must be wary of making rash attacks, Tom. Do not allow yourself to become frustrated. Defend yourself without giving ground and bide your time.'

'Yes, sir,' said Tom.

'But do not bide too much time, of course. You must be bold. Timidity never won a swordfight, Tom. No – it is all about creating the right opportunity. You must gain control of the fight, but by your wits.'

'Yes, sir,' said Tom again. 'But I fear I should be dead before I have a chance to gain control of any swordfight.'

Dr Harker laughed as a light drizzle began to fall from the dark clouds above them. 'Dear me,' he said. 'This will not do, Tom. I shall have to cheer you up. Give me a moment to fetch my wig and we shall away to The Quill where I shall buy you a large bowl of chocolate. How does that sound?'

'It sounds very generous of you, sir.'

'I shall see you at the front door, then. I won't be a moment.'

As the doctor went upstairs, Tom put his coat on and stood in front of the hall mirror. He mimed some fencing moves. He lunged and parried, then stood looking at himself, trying to see the dignified young man he might one day be. Then he noticed Mary the maid standing with one eyebrow raised.

'Mary,' said Tom, coming to a sudden halt and readjusting his coat.

'Master Tom,' she said, walking through to the kitchen with a giggle.

It was the end of September 1716. The summer had been so dry in London that it had been possible – if a little hazardous – to walk across the river beneath the arches of London Bridge, the water level being so low.

The smell from the Thames and from the Fleet Ditch had been a nauseating mix of dung heap and fish stall. It had taken a perfumed handkerchief and strong stomach simply to walk about the town.

Now the skies were leaden. It had rained on and off for days, the gutters turning into miniature torrents, their cargo of dead rats and dung, newspapers and rotten vegetables, sailing away on the rapids.

Ladies busied themselves with preventing their expensive silk dresses from trailing in puddles or being splashed by passing carriages and horses, hitching their hemlines up as high above their ankles as they dared and picking their way across the slippery rain-soaked cobbles.

It was at times like this, when the grey clouds of autumn closed like a lid over the city, plunging it into a permanent twilight, that Tom felt most strongly the urge to escape and go adventuring.

A pigeon took off from the sign outside The

Quill coffee house as Tom and the doctor approached. Arriving early enough to find that their usual seats by the fire were still vacant, they ordered their coffee and chocolate and Tom tried to go over the swordfighting lesson in his mind while Dr Harker looked at the newspaper. He was vowing to himself to do better next time when Dr Harker suddenly stopped what he was doing and started patting his pockets, searching for something.

'Ah! I almost forgot,' he said finally, pulling a folded piece of paper from his waistcoat pocket. 'I have had a letter from the son of an old friend of mine who died some two years ago now. Walter Gibbs was my friend's name . . . a fine man, Tom. We met at university. His father was a wealthy merchant and before Walter inherited the business, we travelled the world together aboard his father's ships. He was good company, Tom. You would have liked him, I think.'

'I'm sure I would, sir,' said Tom. 'Did he live in London?'

'No, no,' said Dr Harker. 'He was a Norfolk man. He came to London when he had to, but always reluctantly. He was immensely proud of Norfolk and I am ashamed to say that I never did get to his house there, despite frequent invitations.'

'And do you know his son, sir?'

'Yes,' the doctor said. 'His name is Abraham and his father was very proud of him, I know. I promised Walter that I would keep in contact with his son, and generally take an interest in his affairs, and I have done so. Abraham lived in Bristol until his father died, then he moved to the family home in Norfolk. We try to meet whenever business brings him to London and I am happy to say that a relationship that was born out of a sense of debt to Abraham's father has flowered into a firm friendship. We share many interests and he is passionate about the history of England, and of his beloved Norfolk in particular. Which brings me to this letter, Tom.'

'Yes, sir?'

'What say you to an expedition into the county of East Anglia? I know it is not quite the adventure you hope for . . .'

'I would like to, sir,' said Tom. 'Very much.'

East Anglia may not have been the East Indies, but since Tom had barely stepped out of the shadow of St Paul's, any travel seemed alive with possibilities for adventure.

'Splendid!' exclaimed Dr Harker. 'Abraham has invited me to come and visit and to meet his wife – he is recently married – and I intend to accept. I would greatly appreciate your company.'

'Thank you, sir,' said Tom. 'You have not met his wife before?'

'No, Tom. They were married only last year. Abraham tells me she is very beautiful and very intelligent. There speaks a man in love, eh, Tom?' Tom smiled and blushed a little. 'But there is another reason to tempt us to make the long journey, Tom. Abraham says that he has some artefacts that may interest me . . .' Dr Harker searched through the letter. 'Ah . . . yes . . . here we are: "I have recently excavated a nearby burial mound dating from the time of the ancient warrior kings of East Anglia. I think you will find the artefacts and the legend attached to them most diverting . . ." It sounds intriguing, does it not?'

Tom nodded. 'It certainly does, sir.'

'Then I shall reply at once,' said Dr Harker. 'It will be good to get the soot of London from our lungs for a while.'

2

KING'S LYNN

So it was that, a few weeks later, towards the end of October, Tom found himself looking out of a carriage window as rain and wind rattled the glass and did its best to rob him of any view. The cold and damp seemed to have crept into his bones and he had not been able to warm himself for hours. Dr Harker by contrast dozed contentedly, as did most of his fellow passengers, one of whom in particular – a red-faced young draper from Cambridge – seemed to think of Tom as his own personal cushion.

As cold as he was, though, Tom had found the journey fascinating. Desperate not to miss anything of interest, his face glued to the window of the carriage, it had taken him a little while to relax. His recent encounter with the skull-faced highwayman, the White Rider, had made Tom uncomfortably conscious of the threat of being attacked by robbers, but their coach was thankfully spared any such incident.

Theirs was not an uninterrupted journey however. The coach had become stuck in mud, the rim trapped behind a large stone in the rutted lane, and then it lost a wheel while being freed. There was much grumbling among the passengers and Dr Harker led a rant about the detestable road conditions in England.

There were many *Hear! Hear!s* and much grumbling about taxes. The wheel took the best part of a day to mend and forced them to make an extra overnight stay in a very uncomfortable and expensive inn.

Consequently they were a day late when their carriage rumbled through a great stone gateway into the town of King's Lynn. Dr Harker had already arranged by letter for them to stay there at the Duke's Head.

The carriage entered the cobbled courtyard of the inn and came to a clattering halt. There followed the usual commotion as the drivers jumped down, coach and horses were led away, hallos were shouted and servants from the inn clambered up to fetch and carry bags.

The inn wrapped itself around the courtyard and Tom and the doctor were led to their rooms, up a flight of stairs and along a wooden gallery that ran all around the yard.

'Cock-fighting at the end there this evening, if you're the betting kind,' said the servant carrying their bags.

'No, thank you,' said Dr Harker.

'It's a very gentlemanly game we run here, sir,' continued the servant. 'We have no trouble to speak of, and what trouble we have is dealt with right speedily and with only whatever knocking of heads is necessary.'

'Thank you again,' said Dr Harker. 'But no. We will be wanting something to eat, however. Can you recommend somewhere in the vicinity?'

'There's no finer place to eat in Lynn, sir, than this very establishment, they say. That's the truth and I swear it. The dining room is just past the stairs we came up. Now, sirs, here we are. I hope you'll both be comfortable.'

'I'm sure we shall,' said Dr Harker, looking through the open door of one of the rooms they had just arrived at. 'Here's something for your trouble.'

'Thank you kindly, sir,' said the servant, pocketing the coin Dr Harker had just given him. 'Are you in the town on business, sir?'

'No, not really,' said the doctor. 'We are visiting a friend.'

'Here in Lynn, sir?'

'No, in Brandham,' said Dr Harker. 'Do you know the place?'

'Aye, sir. My sister is a maid in a house over

that way. There are some strange folk up there on the coast, sir, if you'll let me tell you that.'

'Strange?' said Dr Harker with a smile. 'In what way strange?'

'Strange as in devil-worshipping heathens, sir.' Tom stared at Dr Harker. 'There's one up there who'd be hanged as a wizard if it weren't that he was a lord.'

'We are to be guests of Mr Abraham Gibbs of Low House,' said Dr Harker. 'I trust he is not one of your devil-worshippers?'

'Mr Gibbs, is it?' said the servant with a look of great seriousness. 'No. He's no heathen to my knowledge. But there are things that ought to be held up and looked at and there's things that are best left alone, if you want my opinion. You take care, sirs, is all I'll say. It's a different land up there.'

Dr Harker chuckled, but the servant did not alter his expression.

'Is there something you wish to say about Mr Gibbs?' the doctor asked, seeing that he had caused offence.

'I'm sure it's none of my business,' said the

servant abruptly. 'Now if you'll excuse me, gentlemen.' He eyed them both warily, bowed and left at some speed, leaving Tom and Dr Harker looking at each other in amused bafflement.

Tom shook his head and went through to his room, putting his bags down and looking around. The walls were panelled with dark wood, but they were comfortable enough and after a maid breezed in cheerily to light a fire, a warm glow made it seem very cosy indeed.

Having settled themselves in, Tom and Dr Harker walked down to the dining room and ordered some food. The meal was every bit as good as the servant had promised it would be, and though they had intended to take a stroll about the town, neither Tom nor Dr Harker had the energy for it.

As they headed back to their rooms the cock-fighting was underway. They could hear the cheers and curses of the gamblers through the door. A burly man standing guard tipped his hat to them as they passed. A great cheer rose up again from inside like the roar of an animal.

The food and the journey had worked their magic on Tom and within minutes of saying goodnight to Dr Harker, and within seconds of checking his bed for lice, he was in a deep and dreamless sleep.

3

THE SMUGGLER

The following morning, Dr Harker rapped on Tom's door. Tom was already awake and dressed and together they went downstairs for breakfast. As they drank their coffee, Dr Harker saw the innkeeper and attracted his attention.

'My young friend and I would like to take a coach to Brandham,' said Dr Harker. 'Could you arrange that for us?'

'No, sir,' stated the man matter-of-factly. 'I could not.'

'I beg your pardon,' said Dr Harker. 'Are you saying there is no coach that will take us to Brandham or are you saying you will not arrange it?'

'Oh, there is a coach, sir,' said the man. 'And ordinarily I would be only too happy to oblige.'

'Ordinarily?' queried Dr Harker, trying not to get annoyed. 'And what may I ask makes today extraordinary?'

In answer the man opened the front door of the inn. A cacophony of sounds burst in like a pack of dogs after a fox. Through the open door, Tom and the doctor could see a rich confusion of colour and movement.

'It's Tuesday!' the man shouted by way of explanation.

'Tuesday?' Dr Harker shouted back.

'Market day,' said the man, closing the door. 'There's a coach all right. But you won't get on it;

not this morning at any rate. But why the hurry? You are welcome to stay another night, gentlemen.'

'No thank you,' said Doctor Harker. 'Your accommodation is excellent and we have been most comfortable. But we really must press on to Brandham. Is there nothing you can do?'

'Well, sir,' said the man, 'I wouldn't want it said I wouldn't help a gentlemen who needs it. You are determined to leave this morning? Leave it with me and I'll see what can be done. Come back at ten o'clock.'

'Very well,' said Dr Harker. 'In the meantime we'll see what this fine town has to offer for our amusement.'

'As you wish, sir,' said the man. 'But hold onto your purse and your sword hilt. They'll have the coat off your back if you ain't wary, sir.'

Tom and Dr Harker entered the crowd like small boats launching into the breakers of a choppy sea. Tom endeavoured to keep as close as he could to Dr Harker and his sword, for though the market was no busier than those in London, it seemed foreign and strange to him, with accents so thick he barely recognized the language as English.

The square was skirted with fine houses and inns and at one end of the market stood a great wooden market cross, newly built and very grand. It was domed, rather like a miniature St Paul's, with columns beneath. There were wooden market stalls in front of it and butchers' shambles on either side, casting the heavy scent of raw meat about the square. Tom and the doctor walked through the town until they reached the river.

'The Great Ouse,' said Dr Harker, lingering on the pronunciation of Ouse so that it came out as 'oooooze'. 'What a wonderful name, eh, Tom?' Tom smiled a crooked smile. The name seemed wholly appropriate to the cold, milky, silt-clouded expanse of water.

Tom loved the bustle of the docks in London, and though much smaller, there was no less activity here. Barrels of wine and bulging sacks of corn were being loaded and unloaded and smells of soap, tobacco and fish fought for dominance as they walked along the quay.

Sailors shouted and sang at their work, bound together in that strange seaborne brotherhood that seemed to encompass every nation on earth. Tom was filled with his usual urge to hop aboard and join them, to sail away to the worlds that seemed forever locked away from him.

He then became aware of a strange noise above the clamour of the quayside. A few of the sailors paused in their work to look towards the sound. Then, clenching their teeth tightly about their pipe stems, they returned to their work.

The noise was a rumbling, creaking sound, interrupted occasionally by a sharp CRACK and a shout. Tom and the doctor walked away from the quayside and the sound grew louder until, as they walked to the end of one of the alleys lined with warehouses, they met the source of the noise.

Turning a corner they saw in front of them the Customs House. A fellow passenger had identified it as they had arrived and Dr Harker had been full of praise for the sophistication of its design. But the scene before them was somewhat less than sophisticated.

A horse and cart was being led past the Customs House. Tied to the back of the cart by his wrists was a man, stripped to the waist. Behind him another man followed with a whip already soaked in blood. The man's back was as red and raw as the meat in the shambles.

Tom had seen this punishment before, of course. Being whipped through the streets was not an unusual sight in London. But what seemed strange here was that few people cheered as the man was struck and many more looked on in hard-mouthed silence.

'What is the man's crime?' asked Dr Harker of a merchant standing nearby.

'He is a smuggler,' said the man.

'And is he a popular man, then?' said Dr Harker, indicating the lack of response to the man's punishment.

'He is a smuggler,' repeated the man with a shrug. 'People hereabouts have a certain respect for smugglers, reprehensible though that surely is.'

'Respect?'

'Well, sir,' said the man. 'I'm a law-abiding man, of course. But there are those who feel the duties the government has put on coffee and brandy and such-like necessities of life are enough to turn a man to doing business with the likes of young Ned Sawyer there . . . If that indeed be his name. Good day to you, sir.' The man tipped his hat and moved away.

The cart, the bound man and the whip's cracking moved away and the sound became quiet enough so that Tom did not feel the need to blink each time. The townsfolk carried on watching for a while and then returned to their respective businesses.

By the time they returned to the Duke's Head, the innkeeper had arranged their transport. Dr Harker was very grateful, until he saw the vehicle that was to take them to Brandham. It was a farm cart, piled with sacks.

'I know it ain't much,' said the innkeeper. 'But it's the best I can do. Joe here can take you to the door.'

'Well,' said Dr Harker, 'I suppose we must be grateful we have transport of any kind.' He took out his purse but the innkeeper waved his money away.

'No, no, sir,' he said. 'No need for that now. I wouldn't see you stranded, sir, and Joe here will accept no fee. He does it from Christian duty, that's all, sir.' Joe nodded.

'We are very grateful,' said Dr Harker.

'Yes,' said Tom. 'Thank you.'

'I'm afraid there is only room for one up front with Joe,' said the innkeeper.

Dr Harker looked at Tom and Tom smiled.

'I shall be fine in the back,' he said, climbing onto the sacks.

'Very well,' said Dr Harker to the innkeeper. 'We shall bid you good day, sir.' He climbed up next to the farmer.

'Good journey to you both,' said the innkeeper. 'I'll see you Saturday, Joe.'

'Saturday,' said the farmer and waved. 'Giddup.' He turned to Dr Harker as they pulled away. 'That's cold,' he said.

'Yes,' said Dr Harker. 'Yes it is.' And that was the extent of their conversation for the entire trip.

* * *

The journey from King's Lynn to Brandham was slow, but not as uncomfortable as Tom had feared. The sacks of grain in the cart provided a reasonable seat and luckily, though cold, it was a sunny morning with frost glowing cobalt-blue in the hedges and tree shadows, and in the corners of fields where the sun was yet to make itself felt.

Tom concentrated on drinking in the view, seeing further than he had seen in all his days in London. It was not long before they seemed to have left all civilization behind them, with barely a sign of habitation visible.

Tom saw the battlements of an ancient castle at one point, and there were scattered cottages with smoke rising from their chimneys and workers in the fields. There were others on the road too, walking or riding home from the market. Church towers and windmills broke the horizon.

At one point the route took them up a long hill, the lane bounded on both sides by hedges filled with red berries. The birds that were feeding on them rose up in a great flock as they approached. Crows and rooks stood out black against the brown earth like currants in a cake.

At a crossroads at the top of the hill, Dr Harker tapped Tom on the shoulder and there in the distance Tom saw the sea; wide and shining under a clear blue sky. Light played among the inlets of a huge expanse of marshland and lit up the white dunes beyond. The scene was laid out like a painting, the horizon unbroken wherever he looked, the sunlight glinting on a weather vane to his right, great ships reduced to toys by distance.

'Well, Tom?' Dr Harker called out, turning in his seat. 'That's a view that's worth the effort, eh?'

'Yes, sir!' Tom shouted back. 'It is!'

The cart clattered on its way steadily down the hill. Tom could see the village at the end of the lane and in no time at all dolls' houses turned into real houses, of stone, of brick and of flint.

The cart turned off the village street, clattered past two huge gateposts – each with a stone globe on top – and drove down a long gravel drive edged by lime trees. Tom turned to face forwards to see where they were going and caught his first view of Low House, which was now only a hundred yards ahead.

The house was much grander than Tom had expected. He had been envisaging some ancient old country hall, but this was a large two-storey house with high brick walls and large windows. There was an imposing doorway with columns either side, and a wide flight of stone steps leading up to it. Tom and Dr Harker hopped down from the cart onto the first step.

'Thank you, Mr . . . Joe,' said Dr Harker. Their driver gave them a brief nod of farewell, clucked his teeth and flicked the reins, setting the cart in motion once again.

'I had no idea Gibbs had such a fine house,' said Dr Harker. 'No wonder his father was so proud of it.'

'It is very fine,' said Tom. 'Mr Gibbs must be very wealthy.'

Dr Harker smiled. 'Very,' he said. 'Abraham comes from a long line of very successful merchants, Tom.'

Soon the rattling cart was gone and Tom was amazed by the silence that enveloped them. Apart from the odd twitter or chirrup, there was no sound at all. After a life lived in London, it was a little unnerving. Dr Harker walked up and rapped on the front door, but there was no response.

'How very odd,' he said. 'There should be someone about.'

Just at that moment, they heard footsteps approaching behind them from the road they had just travelled along.

Up the drive walked a slow procession of figures.

4

LOW HOUSE

The group was downcast and solemn, one of the women crying openly and being comforted by another. As they approached, one of the men walked away from the group and over towards Tom and the doctor.

'Dr Harker,' he said, making an attempt at a smile and holding out his hand.

'Abraham,' said Dr Harker. 'We were delayed.' The rest of the party walked to the back of the house. As they walked past Tom, the woman comforting the crying woman looked right at him and for some reason her gaze unsettled him.

'This must be your assistant,' said Abraham Gibbs, holding his hand out to Tom.

'Yes, sir,' said Tom. 'I am very pleased to make your acquaintance.'

'And I yours,' said Gibbs. 'But I'm afraid you arrive at an unfortunate time, gentlemen. As you can see, we are just returned from a funeral. It is a very sad business, I'm afraid.'

'If there is a problem, I am sure that Tom and I could find accommodation elsewhere . . .'

'No, no,' said Gibbs. 'Not another word of it. Forgive me, gentlemen. You have had a long and tiring journey and this is the welcome that awaits you. There is no reason at all for you to consider staying elsewhere and besides, my wife would never hear of it. She has been looking forward to your arrival for weeks. It is just that . . .' Gibbs broke off and took a deep breath. 'It is just that there has been a tragic accident and it has unsettled the household, as I am sure you will understand. Please come inside out of the cold. Foley will take your bags.'

Tom noticed a man standing at his shoulder. The suddenness of his appearance made him take a step back. Foley was a good few inches taller than Tom and much thicker-set. His face was gaunt, his eyes set deep into his skull and overshadowed by thick eyebrows that seemed fixed in an expression of distrustful scrutiny.

In contrast to his thin face, Foley's lips were thick and fleshy, turned down at the sides in a permanent expression of slight disgust. They gave him, Tom thought, the unpleasant look of a codfish.

Tom handed his bag to Foley and Dr Harker followed suit. Foley took them without a word, lifting them as if they were weightless. The only acknowledgment he offered was the slightest of nods before turning and walking away towards the house.

Gibbs noticed the glance that Dr Harker and Tom exchanged.

'You mustn't mind Foley,' he said in a conspiratorial whisper. 'He is wary, that is all. He is a good man.'

'Wary?' said Dr Harker. 'Wary of what?'

'Of everything and everybody,' said Gibbs with a wry smile.

They followed Gibbs up the flight of stone steps and in through the front door of the house. They walked through a wide tiled hallway with a grand staircase leading up from it and into a large room that overlooked a lawn and some clipped yews. At the end of the lawn was a low wall and beyond that a wild expanse of salt marshes.

'What an extraordinary view,' said Dr Harker. 'Is it not, Tom?'

Tom agreed that it was, but he was realizing that it was not the landscape that was so overwhelming, but rather the vast uninterrupted skyscape above it.

'I love it,' said Gibbs. 'Especially this part of the coast. To the east and west much of the land has been reclaimed from the sea, protected by dykes, but here we have tidal marshes.

'Some would call it bleak, but I think it the most beautiful sight in all England,' he continued proudly. They stood in silence for a moment, staring out at the cloud shadows moving across the sunlit marshes. Dr Harker was the first to speak.

'But what of the accident you mentioned?' he said. 'Mrs Gibbs is not hurt, I hope?'

'No,' said Gibbs. 'Susannah is quite unharmed, though she has been badly shaken by what has happened. I am sorry, Josiah. Of course, you still have not been introduced. Susannah was comforting one of the other servants. It was a young maid – Margaret Dereham – whose funeral we were attending just now.'

'How did the poor girl die?'

'I'm afraid Margaret fell victim to the marshes. The creeks are a death trap, my friends. The locals know the dangers – and the safe routes through – but you must promise me that you will not venture into them unguided.'

'But what are the dangers?' asked Tom, still a little unclear as to how the maid had died.

'The mud, Tom,' said Gibbs. 'The creeks are filled with a shifting sandy mud that may appear solid – may even *be* solid – at one moment, and then be the consistency of molasses the next. It sucks you down and your feet can find no purchase with which to push yourself upward. Within seconds, the strongest man in England would not be able to pull himself free. It is a horrible death.' Tom looked back towards the marshes and the cloud shadows suddenly seemed darker to him.

'But was Margaret not a local girl?' queried Dr Harker. 'Was she not aware of the dangers?'

'Born and bred not half a mile from here,' said Gibbs. He sighed. 'I can offer no explanation for it at all, I'm afraid. Please, won't you sit down?'

He showed Tom and the doctor to a small group of chairs placed in front of a huge stone fireplace and all three sat down. A log fire blazed in the hearth and Tom noticed that the firedogs supporting the grate were fashioned into fierce dragonheads, snaking forward as if about to bite their ankles. Their shadows shivered and twisted by the firelight. Gibbs saw Tom's expression and smiled.

'They were a wedding present from a rather eccentric neighbour of ours,' he said. 'Susannah loathes them, but I must say I've grown rather fond of them.'

'You were telling us about the accident,' said Dr Harker.

'Yes,' said Gibbs. 'The truly dreadful thing is that Margaret came to her end only a matter of a few dozen yards from the house.'

'And nothing could be done?' said Tom.

'Foley heard screams but by the time he arrived, the mud had already closed over Margaret's head. A few strands of hair were the only sign that she was even there. Foley tried to ford the creek to aid her, but began to sink himself. Had help not arrived, he might also have been taken. It took Foley and two other men to lift Margaret clear using a garden rake they found nearby. She was dead by the time they pulled her free.'

'But what was Margaret doing there in the first

place? Do any of her duties take her to the creek?'

'No, none at all,' said Gibbs. He looked off in the direction of the marsh. 'Strange to say, Margaret seemed to have an odd obsession with the marshes.'

'How so?' asked Dr Harker.

'Well, I had often seen her standing there of late, looking out across the creeks. Almost as if she were looking for something.'

'Looking for something?'

'Maybe,' said Gibbs. 'But this is foolishness. Maybe I am starting to believe this nonsense myself.'

'What nonsense is that, sir?' said Tom.

'I see Abraham has not yet told you the whole story.'

All three turned at the sound of the voice.

'Susannah!' said Gibbs. 'I thought you were going to remain in your bed until you felt stronger.' Tom and Dr Harker got to their feet.

'And miss the chance of diverting company?' his wife replied.

Susannah Gibbs walked towards them from the relative shadow of the doorway, into the warm glow of the firelight. She was wearing a pale silk dress that flickered with the borrowed light from the candles and the fire until it looked as though she had brought her own illumination with her.

'You must be the illustrious Doctor Harker whom Abraham has told me so much about,' she said.

'I am delighted to meet you,' said Dr Harker. 'Abraham was trying to convince us that the view across the marshes was the most beautiful in England. I fear he may need spectacles.'

Mrs Gibbs smiled. 'You flatter me, Dr Harker. But one can never have enough flattery. And who is this handsome young man?'

She turned to Tom. The candlelight sparkled in her pale green eyes; the same eyes which had studied Tom as she had walked past comforting the maid when they had arrived. She was without question the most beautiful woman Tom had ever seen.

'This,' said Dr Harker, seeing that Tom was not going to reply, 'is my assistant, Thomas Marlowe.'

'How do you do?' said Tom, finally finding his voice.

'Very well, thank you, Mr Marlowe,' said Mrs Gibbs. 'Shall we all sit down?'

'You alluded to something when you came in, Mrs Gibbs,' said Dr Harker when Mrs Gibbs had sat down and they could all return to their chairs. 'You said that Abraham had not told us the *whole* story. What did you mean by that?'

'Come now, Susannah,' said Gibbs firmly. 'I must insist. We agreed that—'

'*You* agreed, my dear,' said Susannah.

'But it is just foolish village talk,' insisted Gibbs. 'I will not have it in the house.'

'Maybe so,' said his wife a little more forcefully. 'But after what has happened to poor Margaret, I hope you will allow me to take a particular interest in such matters. You may find it easy to dismiss tales of curses and the like but you are a man and men are such cold-blooded creatures. Oh, I think I must retire to my room. I am so sorry . . .'

With this, Mrs Gibbs rose from her chair and, holding a handkerchief to her face, she turned and walked swiftly towards the door, her husband in pursuit.

'Susannah,' Gibbs cried out. 'For pity's sake. Why do you insist on upsetting yourself like this?'

5

THE MARSH

'I am beginning to think that another night in King's Lynn would not have been so terrible after all, eh, Tom?' said Dr Harker. Tom was about to reply when he was interrupted by the return of Abraham Gibbs.

'You must forgive Susannah,' he said.

'There is nothing to forgive,' said Dr Harker. 'She is upset and has good cause, it seems. You have a lovely wife, sir. You are a fortunate man.'

Gibbs gave a weary smile and, picking up a poker, prodded at the burning logs. 'I should be,' he said. 'I certainly should be.'

'Why only "should"?' said Dr Harker. 'This incident with the servant is tragic, but is there something else bothering you? A problem shared is often a problem solved.'

'Very well,' said Gibbs, laying down the poker and sitting once more to face Tom and the doctor, his face lit by the fire, his eyes flickering with the reflection of its flames. 'Susannah has begun so I may as well follow.'

'What is it?' asked Dr Harker gently.

'We are very cut off from the world here, gentlemen. King's Lynn is thriving and I am confident it will one day surpass even Norwich in importance. But here among the country folk of Norfolk, things take a little longer to change. There is foolish talk among the local people and indeed some of our own servants that

Margaret's death was not an accident at all.'

'They think it was murder?' said Dr Harker with a frown.

'Of a kind,' said Gibbs with a sigh. 'It has to do with a local legend.'

'Which is?'

Gibbs lifted a log and tossed it onto the fire before replying, 'It is the legend of the Sentinel.'

'The Sentinel?' asked Tom. 'What is the Sentinel, sir?'

'The Sentinel is really only a local scare tale to keep children out of the marshes,' said Gibbs. He saw that Tom and Dr Harker were not going to be satisfied with that and sighed as he reluctantly continued. 'Locals will have you believe that a ghoul called the Sentinel stalks the creeks, keeping watch on Redwulf's grave.'

'Redwulf?' Tom queried.

'Yes,' said Gibbs. 'It is his burial chamber that I have been studying. Redwulf was one of the ancient Anglo-Saxon warrior kings. As you no doubt know, the Angles and Saxons were our ancestors and invaded this land from the Continent after the collapse of the Roman

Empire. The fine villas and temples of the Romans were shunned and left to crumble, while they were replaced by timber halls where tales would be told by flickering firelight of gods and demons, heroes and dragons. Redwulf himself has attracted a good deal of local legends – in particular this legend concerning the guardian of his grave. They say that the grave is cursed; that anyone who seeks to desecrate it will suffer the wrath of the Sentinel.

'It is foolishness, of course, but it has had an unsettling effect on Susannah and I have forbidden any mention of it in this house. I would ask you to humour me in this respect. The servants are like children, Josiah. They will hang on to these fairy stories.'

'Tom and I shall do nothing to upset Mrs Gibbs or your household, I hope,' said Dr Harker.

'Thank you,' said Gibbs. 'I apologize if I seem a bore about this, but it is for the best. If truth be told, I think the smugglers hereabouts are to blame for the myth of a curse on the grave.'

'How so?' said Dr Harker.

'Well, Josiah, they feed the legend to keep prying eyes away from their activities,' said Gibbs. 'It suits their purpose only too well. Further along the coast they talk of a ghostly lantern-eyed hound. The only lanterns shining along the coast at night are those of the smuggling fraternity, my friends, I promise you.' Dr Harker nodded. 'Their nocturnal activities among the creeks hereabouts keep the legend alive. It seems that the locals are happier to believe that a figure they see in the marshes is a spectre rather than the far more likely figure of a smuggler. Ordinarily these tales do not bother me, but now they are upsetting Susannah and that is why I have banned their mention in the house.'

Tom could not stop himself turning to look back towards the window. Twilight was dimly falling and Tom yearned suddenly for the comforting familiarity of the London streets.

'I am sorry to make you speak further on this subject,' said Dr Harker, 'but I still do not see the connection with the maidservant, Abraham. She had no reason to fear this Sentinel, imaginary or not. She had not disturbed the grave. Why would anyone believe her to be cursed?'

Gibbs looked at him and leaned back in his chair.

'Well,' he said, 'the strange thing is, Josiah, that they found something on Margaret's body . . .'

'Found something?'

'A piece of jewellery,' said Gibbs. 'A bracelet. She was wearing a bracelet.'

'And this bracelet. It came from the grave goods?'

'From the grave, yes,' said Gibbs. 'I have hired an artist to draw the finds and he left them unattended for a while. When he returned they were gone. I hesitate to speak ill of the dead, but Margaret must have stolen them. Though I must own that I have no notion as to why she would do such a thing. The bracelet was interesting in terms of our history, Josiah, but it was of little or no value to Margaret. Besides, Susannah was very fond of Margaret and treated her very well. I often warned that she was being too familiar with her, but they were of similar ages and I could see that they enjoyed to chatter. I could not begrudge Susannah that feminine company so far from society as we are here. But my worries seem to have been confirmed because despite the fact that Susannah would give Margaret all manner of presents – she was wearing one of Susannah's old cloaks when she died – we then discover that the girl was stealing from us. And a theft in the house is a distressing business, as you no doubt know. It creates a poisonous atmosphere.' Dr Harker nodded.

'Margaret's death was a tragedy, but that is not enough for some people. Once the word got out that she had been found with an item from the burial, the feeble-minded hereabouts decided that the Sentinel must have attacked her.'

'But I got the impression that there was more,' said Dr Harker.

Gibbs sighed. 'Yes, Josiah,' he said. 'You are right, of course. It is not simply that people believe the Sentinel guards the barrow. There is also a lot of local resentment about my excavation of the burial. Susannah was attacked in the street by a group of villagers only last week.'

'Attacked?'

'Yes,' said Gibbs. 'Only verbally, thank

goodness. A group of local people confronted her when she was riding through the village and shouted abuse, demanding that the grave goods be returned to the barrow. And then only days later, Margaret is found in the creek. It has been a hellish few days, Josiah.' Gibbs bowed his head and rubbed the tips of his fingers into his forehead.

'Tom,' said Dr Marlowe. 'Be a good fellow and fetch Abraham a brandy. I think I see some over there.'

Tom stood up and walked across to the small table by the window and poured some brandy into one of the glasses. As he picked it up to carry it back, he looked out of the window towards the marsh and saw a figure standing among the creeks watching the house.

'Tom?' said Dr Harker. Tom turned to the sound of the voice and then back to the window. When he looked back to the marsh the figure was gone.

'Tom?' said Dr Harker again. 'The brandy? Are you quite all right?'

'Yes . . . Yes, sir,' he said, walking back

towards the fire. 'Sorry. Here you are, Mr Gibbs. This might make you feel a little better.' He looked nervously back towards the window.

'Tom?' said Dr Harker.

'It's nothing sir, really.'

'What?' said Gibbs as if he had forgotten they were even there and seemingly noticing the drink for the first time. 'Oh, yes, thank you. You're very kind.' He drank the glass back in one go and took a deep breath. 'There is more, gentlemen. If you'll follow me . . .'

Tom and Dr Harker followed Gibbs as he rose from his chair and left the room, walking through the hall, past the staircase and leaving the house by the garden door. They followed past the clipped hedges and down the brick path to the gate that led through the low wall to the marsh.

The gate opened with a cat-like mew and, once through, Gibbs stopped with his back to the creeks and pointed at the wall in front of him. 'This appeared this morning. These words and words like them have appeared almost every day since I took the artefacts from the burial chamber.'

Tom looked to where his host was pointing. There on the wall, scratched feverishly into the ginger-coloured stonework, over and over again, were the words:

'*Return it* '.

6

REDWULF'S SWORD

Tom pulled the curtains to in his room. He could see nothing through the window except the ghostly reflection of his own pale face in the glass, but it was that nothingness he found so unsettling. The view was as black as if the windows had been boarded up.

'It is a place to chill the blood, is it not?' said a voice behind him. Standing in the doorway, leaning against the jam, was a man whom Tom guessed to be about thirty years old. He was shorter than Tom, even taking into consideration the height of his wig, and a little stout. As he spoke, he crossed himself.

'Allow me to introduce myself,' he said with a strong accent Tom did not recognize. 'My name is Michaelangelo Bamberini.' He walked into the room, holding out his hand which Tom shook.

'Tom Marlowe,' said Tom. 'Are you a guest here also, Mister . . .?'

'Bamberini,' the man repeated. 'In a manner of speaking, yes. Signor Gibbs has asked me to make drawings of these things he has found.'

'Yes. The artefacts from the burial mound,' said Tom.

'Art-e-facts. Exactly so,' said Bamberini. 'You must excuse me. My English is not so good.'

'Your English is excellent, sir,' asked Tom. 'Are you Spanish?' he continued, instantly regretting the question as he saw Bamberini's face turn scarlet.

'Spanish?!' squawked Bamberini putting his hand to his heart as if Tom had struck him. '*Spanish? Madonna!*'

'I'm sorry,' said Tom. 'I . . . I . . . I didn't mean to offend you.' Bamberini fanned himself with a silk handkerchief and seemed to calm down a little. His outburst had attracted Dr Harker's attention and he came from his room to see what was happening.

'Is everything all right, Tom?' asked the doctor.

'Yes, Dr Harker. That is, I hope so. I have given offence without meaning to. This is Mister Bambear-eenee.'

'Signor Michaelangelo Bamberini at your service, sir,' the artist said with a bow.

'Dr Josiah Harker, at yours,' said the doctor with a smile. 'And how has Tom here offended you?'

'He meant no harm, I am sure,' said Bamberini. 'I know the English know of nothing outside of their beloved little island, so it should come as little surprise that I, a Tuscan, a citizen of Firenze – Florence you call her – a city so beautiful that it would burn your eyes to look on it after your . . .' – he rubbed the ends of his fingers together and pursed his lips in disgust – 'your King's Lynns and your Londons; that I, Michaelangelo Antonio Giaccomo Bamberini, should be mistaken for a *Spaniard*!'

Tom opened his mouth to speak, but Bamberini held up his hand and closed his eyes.

'Please do not try to apologize again, I beg of you. Bamberini accepts your apology. None further is needed. You are English and therefore know little of the world. Here is my hand, sir. There, we are friends.'

With that he turned and left the room, leaving Tom and the doctor staring open-mouthed after him.

'What a wonderfully annoying little man,' said Dr Harker, smiling. 'I rather think dinner is unlikely to be a relaxing affair, Tom.'

'I agree, sir,' said Tom.

'But to be serious,' said Dr Harker. 'I had the feeling that there was something disturbing you when we were downstairs. You seemed distracted.'

'There was something,' said Tom. 'But I hardly know what to make of it.'

'Yes?' The doctor closed the door and moved closer to Tom.

'When we first arrived,' said Tom, 'I saw something from the window: a figure way off in the distance in the marshes.'

'A figure? In the marshes?' said Dr Harker. 'Could you make out any features of this figure?'

'No, sir,' said Tom. 'It was twilight and it was too far away . . .'

'It?' said Dr Harker. 'I have a feeling you are being influenced by Gibbs's story about the Sentinel, Tom. Could it not have been a local man doing, well, whatever the locals do in these places?'

'No, sir,' said Tom. 'I just . . . I don't know sir. It . . . he . . . was watching the house.'

'Come now, Tom,' said Dr Harker. 'Watching the house or merely *looking* at the house. There might be all kinds of benign reasons for that. The Sentinel story is fascinating, to be sure, but often, as Abraham says, these stories are there to distract the simple-minded. *We* will not be so easy to distract, eh?'

'No, sir,' said Tom, sounding less than sure.

'Splendid. Then I say we away to dinner. I could eat a horse!'

Dinner was more enjoyable than Tom or the doctor had imagined, and afterwards Mrs Gibbs begged their leave to retire as she was feeling tired. They all stood and bid her goodnight and Gibbs poured them all another brandy.

'So tell us more about this Redwulf of yours, Abraham,' said Dr Harker when Bamberini had finished yet another long speech about the beauty of the Tuscan hills.

'Well,' began Gibbs, 'Redwulf was one of the warrior kings of East Anglia in the seventh century, as I have said: a chieftain of the peoples who came to populate this land when the Romans left. Bede's *Ecclesiastical History* mentions him, as do the *Anglo-Saxon Chronicles*. He is always described as being very tall, exceptionally skilled with sword and spear and almost superhumanly strong. He was famed for his quick wits and fearlessness in battle. In fact, he was unbeaten in combat and his eventual death seems to have been as the victim of a plot, poisoned by one of his own guards.'

He unlocked the door and led them all into the library.

'Ever since the theft of part of the hoard,' he explained, 'I have kept the library locked.' Except for two long windows opposite the door, book-cases covered the walls in the room. Dr Harker clicked his tongue in approval.

'This is quite a library, Abraham,' he said.

'Yes,' said Gibbs. 'Yes, I suppose it is. My father's collection really, though I have added one or two volumes. I even have a copy of your book about the Death and the Arrow murders. Quite fascinating. I hope you will sign it for me later, Josiah.'

'I should be honoured,' said Dr Harker, puff-ing out his chest a little. Tom smiled. Gibbs walked over towards the window where there was a table and chair covered with papers, some of which had drawings on them. Next to the table was a huge wooden chest with studded metal clasps and straps and huge hinges. The wood was carved with crude foliate designs and both the wood and the metal were black with age.

Bamberini stood back and looked on with his perpetual expression of boredom as Gibbs crouched down, lifted the lid and took out a large bundle wrapped in muslin, which he gently laid on the floor. He opened up the muslin and flattened it out, arranging the objects it had concealed on the flattened fabric. Tom looked on in wonder at the display of curious objects at his feet, crouching down alongside Gibbs for a closer look. Dr Harker joined them.

There were gold brooches and bracelets covered in complex patterns, some inlaid with semi-precious stones or coloured glass. There was beautiful jewellery with beads of amber and glass. There were decorated cups, bowls and spoons. There were spearheads, a hatchet and a huge knife.

'My word, Abraham,' said Dr Harker. 'I had no idea the items were of this quality.'

'They are extraordinary, aren't they?' said Gibbs.

'I never realized they would be so beautiful,' said Tom.

'The craftsmanship is superb,' said Gibbs.

'Look at this brooch. Look at the fine gold working, the lovely enamelling. Try and find a match
for this now and you would search a long time.'

Dr Harker looked at a nearby table and picked
up a piece of paper. 'And you did these drawings,
Signor?' he asked.

'*Si*,' he said. 'They are Bamberini's.'

'You are very good, aren't you?' said Tom.

'*Si*,' said Bamberini with a smile. 'I am.' Then
as an afterthought: '*Grazie*. That is, thank you.'

'Tom is quite right, Signor,' said Dr Harker.
'These drawings really are very fine. They are not
only accurate as a representation of the finds, but
also beautiful in their own right as works of art.'

'It is not difficult to be inspired with such
craftsmanship to work from,' said Bamberini. 'It
is not so good as Roman work of course, but still,
Bamberini likes them very much.'

'This is perhaps the most evocative of the
finds,' said Gibbs, taking something else out of
the chest. He laid the parcel on the floor and
gently opened it. 'Redwulf's sword!'

Tom stared in wonder at the ancient sword, its
blade blackened and half eaten away, but its hilt

showing the same quality of craftsmanship as the rest of the hoard.

'This is the sword he called "Bone-cracker",' said Gibbs. 'The sword he wielded in countless victories; the sword on which he swore his oath to protect his people from all attackers; the sword with which, legend has it, he once killed a mounted warrior and his horse with a single mighty blow.'

Dr Harker asked if he might pick it up.

'Incredible,' he said, once he had the sword in his hand. 'You can almost feel the man who once held this.' Tom took the sword next and agreed with Dr Harker that holding the sword did forge a link with this long-dead king.

As exciting though the treasure hoard undoubtedly was, Tom began to yawn through the sheer exhaustion of travelling and said that perhaps it was time that he retired to bed. Dr Harker and Gibbs bade him goodnight and Tom went up to his room.

Tom got undressed and put out his candle. He pulled the covers around him and lay thinking about Redwulf and the treasure hoard and then, more troublingly, about the maid and the legend of the Sentinel.

The wind was picking up and he could hear it whistling about the house and garden, shaking the branches of the apple trees and rustling the reeds of the creeks. The chimney sighed and moaned.

Tom was used to London sounds: the nightsoil man's cart and the tapping of the watchmen on their rounds, dogs barking, curses and screams and running footsteps; glass breaking, children crying, constables yelling, a horse's hooves clattering on cobbles.

There seemed a comfort in those noises now. This wind-whistling emptiness disturbed him and he found himself longing for a drunken yell or a cat's meow.

Then, behind the whistling, Tom heard a voice. He thought it a trick of the wind at first, but it was not the whispering of twigs or rushes, but that of a man. He heard the crunch of footsteps on the gravel. Then he heard a sound that chilled his blood – a deep growling groan that sounded neither completely human nor belonging to any animal Tom had ever heard.

He rose from his bed and edged across the coal-black room, feeling his way in the pitch-darkness until his fingers happened upon the fabric of the curtains.

Looking out into the night, Tom could see absolutely nothing at first, but slowly the blackness began to crystallize into dimly recognizable forms: the clipped yews, the garden wall, the path. Then a piece of the blackness broke away and moved off.

A few yards off it turned back towards the house and let out a mournful groan. Tom could not discern any features in the darkness, other than that the figure was human-shaped, though huge. It groaned again, lower this time and then turned to stride away into the marshes. Then he saw a faint light that had been illuminating the gravel near the house disappear as if a candle had just been extinguished inside the house.

7

THE BARROW

Tom woke with a start, forgetting for that instant that he was not in his bed in Fleet Street, and stared around in confusion. He had been dreaming, but the memory of it was slipping away as he became more conscious. He was aware somehow, though, that it had not been a pleasant dream and he was happy to let it go. Then he remembered the mysterious groaning figure in the night and shivered.

He got out of bed. Sunlight was beating against the curtains, eager to get in, and when Tom drew them he had to narrow his eyes against the brightness of the morning. He looked down at the view that had been hidden to him the night before.

There was nothing to show that the scene had held such menace only hours before. The marshland beyond the garden looked beautiful, bathed in the apricot glow of the rising sun. Sea birds flew over the dunes beyond the creeks, barely flapping their wings, their flight rising and falling rhythmically like the swell of the sea in the distance.

'Good morning,' said Tom as he walked into the dining room where Dr Harker, Bamberini and Gibbs were already having breakfast.

'Good morning, Tom,' said Gibbs. 'I trust you slept well.' Foley showed him to a chair.

'Actually,' said Tom, sitting down, 'I heard voices in the night. Outside the house. A strange moaning.' Bamberini crossed himself.

'I do wish you would stop doing that,' said Gibbs, giving Bamberini a withering look before turning back to Tom. 'Voices, you say? Do you know anything about that, Foley?'

'I don't know, sir,' said Foley, licking his lips. 'Perhaps it was the wind, sir.'

'True,' said Gibbs, turning to Tom. 'The wind can play tricks on you here.'

'No, sir,' said Tom. 'I saw the man from my window.'

Bamberini made to cross himself again, but stopped halfway and toyed with his collar instead.

'Bamberini here is as superstitious as an old fisherwoman,' said Gibbs with a smile.

'Maybe,' said Bamberini. 'Maybe not. I am not English. You must forgive me. You English like to pretend there is no evil. I know this. I apologize. But evil is here whether you say so or not.'

Gibbs smiled and shook his head. 'Are you sure you heard nothing, Foley?' he asked again. 'I can't have Bamberini thinking we are at the mercy of evil spirits.'

'Ah, yes, sir,' said Foley after a little pause. 'Now I recall that Sam Fortune delivered the new bridle for Mrs Gibbs's horse, with apologies for the delay.'

'But it must have been near midnight,' said Tom.

'It may have been,' said Foley. 'But when Sam sets to work on something he gets it done and he knew the mistress was waiting.'

'Well, then,' said Gibbs. 'That is settled. A perfectly sensible explanation, is it not, Bamberini?'

'A sensible explanation for what, dear?' said Mrs Gibbs, walking into the room.

'Nothing for you to worry about, Susannah,' her husband said. 'Now I have a favour to ask of you, Josiah.'

'Name it, Abraham,' said the doctor.

'Would you be so kind as to accompany me on an errand of business. There is something I need to attend to; something I have been thinking of doing for some time.' Gibbs looked at his wife and smiled. 'Recent events have increased the urgency for action. Would you mind, Josiah? There are signatures to be witnessed.'

'I would be delighted,' said Dr Harker.

'I can take Tom to the barrow,' said Mrs Gibbs. 'I'm sure he would like to see it.'

Tom agreed, enthusiastically.

'If you are sure, my dear?' said Gibbs.

'We shall be fine,' said Mrs Gibbs. 'You go on and attend to your boring business matters.'

'Needless to say,' said Gibbs, 'for pity's sake, be aware of the dangers of the creeks, my dear.'

'I am not a child, Abraham,' said Mrs Gibbs. 'And neither is Tom. I think we can be left without fear of injuring ourselves. Is that not true, Tom?' Tom looked at Gibbs who smiled at his discomfort.

'I leave my wife in your care, sir,' said Gibbs to Tom. 'Please do not let her persuade you to do anything rash or reckless while I am gone.'

'I shall do my best, sir,' said Tom.

Dr Harker and Gibbs said their farewells as Foley brought the carriage out. Tom and Mrs Gibbs watched from the steps of the house as the carriage rumbled down the drive and out of sight.

'Come and say hello to Raven,' said Mrs Gibbs.

'Raven?'

'Yes, Tom,' she said, walking towards the stables. 'My pride and joy.' At the sound of her voice, a beautiful black horse moved to the door of his stable. Susannah Gibbs rested her face against his cheek and patted his neck.

'He's a fine horse,' said Tom. But as he approached, the horse lurched forward as if trying to bite him.

'Raven!' scolded Susannah. 'Your manners are appalling. Say hello to Mr Marlowe.'

Tom walked forward again, and again the horse lurched at him, flaring his nostrils and snorting, kicking at the inside of the stable door. Susannah chuckled.

'Raven is very protective of me, Tom,' she said. 'Abraham loathes him. Raven will allow no one to ride him – or even saddle him – but me. He is a brute, but I do love him so.' She turned to the horse and frowned. 'Not that that gives you the right to be rude to my friends, Raven. Come,

Tom. Let us leave this bad-tempered fellow and go for our stroll.'

As they walked away, the horse seemed to have understood all that was said and threw himself into a rage, whinnying and kicking at the stable door. Tom hoped that the bolt was strong enough to hold him.

'Ehm . . . how is the new bridle?' he asked as they walked on.

'The new bridle?'

'Yes,' said Tom, not quite knowing why he had started this conversation. 'You have a new bridle for Raven, I believe.'

Mrs Gibbs laughed and Tom blushed. 'I'm sorry, Tom,' she said. 'I don't mean to laugh at you. But I have no new bridle, I'm afraid. There is a confusion somewhere.'

'Sorry,' mumbled Tom nervously. 'I thought . . . that is I . . .'

'Now then,' said Susannah Gibbs, linking her arm through Tom's, 'you don't have to be nervous of me. We shall have a chance to become better acquainted. Tell me all about yourself. Omit no details. I adore details.'

So after a faltering start, Tom told her something of his life, of his friendship with Dr Harker and of their recent adventures. He was just about to tell her of his recent discovery that the man he had always called father was in fact his uncle when they came in sight of the barrow.

Ahead of them, just off the track to the beach, on a piece of higher ground that formed a meadow near the stables was a small rounded hummock covered with weeds and grass. Tom would barely have noticed it if Mrs Gibbs had not pointed it out.

'What has Abraham told you about Redwulf?' said Susannah. Tom began to tell her the history that Gibbs had given them but she clapped her hands together.

'Oh, trust Abraham to tell you all that nonsense,' she said. 'Do you mean to say he has not told you of the curse nor of the Sentinel?'

'A little,' said Tom. 'He does not want it spoken of for fear of upsetting you.'

'Nonsense!' said Susannah. 'He does not want it spoken of because it upsets *him*.'

Tom shrugged. 'He told us that there is a

Sentinel who is supposed to guard the barrow,' he said.

'Yes,' said Mrs Gibbs. 'A knight returning from the Crusades saw a vision of St Felix standing on top of the barrow. The vision told him that Redwulf had converted to Christianity before his death and so his grave should be protected from robbers. The knight swore an oath to devote his life to the protection of the grave and so powerful was that oath that they say the knight never did truly die and that he still guards the barrow to this very day. It's a wonderful story, is it not?'

'I suppose it is, yes.'

'It is so romantic,' said Mrs Gibbs.

Tom smiled. 'Except for the idea that he avenges the thefts,' he said.

'I know,' said Mrs Gibbs, the smile fading on her face. 'Poor Margaret. Some say she was killed; that she did not fall at all, but was murdered.'

'Yes,' said Tom. 'But you can't believe that she was killed by a ghostly knight, surely?'

'I don't know, Tom,' she said. 'Anything seems possible in this godforsaken place sometimes. Let us talk about something else. Ah, here we are.'

At the entrance to the burial chamber were two huge stones, one on either side. Both were encrusted with lichen, daubed over the surface like splashes of cream and yellow paint. Set a little way back was another stone, placed across the others like the lintel of a door.

There was a wrought-iron gate barring the way. Tom peered past it into the blackness. Mrs Gibbs offered Tom a key but when he placed his hands on the gate it opened with a rasp and a squeak.

'How odd,' Susannah Gibbs said. 'Abraham must have forgotten to lock it. That is unlike him. You can go in,' she added with a wry smile. 'It is quite safe. The Sentinel is just a story, you do know that, don't you?'

'Of course,' said Tom, anxious not to betray any of the fear that was welling up inside him. 'I was merely adjusting my eyes to the gloom.'

He ducked under the lintel stone and squeezed himself into the burial mound. There was a drop in level just inside the doorway and Tom almost fell over, stumbling into the heart of the mound far more swiftly than he had intended. There was a dank, mushroom-like taint to the air.

'The bones are at the far end, Tom,' called Mrs Gibbs. 'There is a plank door covered in earth that you can lift out of the way.'

Tom felt his way along to the back of the barrow until he could feel something hollow under his hand. He scraped back some sandy soil and, sure enough, there was a small door lying flat on the earth.

He prised his fingers underneath and lifted it up, aware all of a sudden of a feeling of dread rising up in him at the prospect of viewing the bones of this legendary warrior. But this feeling of trepidation was overtaken by one of surprise.

'There's nothing here!' he shouted. 'The bones have— The bones have *gone*!' There was no reply.

Tom looked towards the entrance and the relative glare made the inside of the barrow seem even darker than before.

'Mrs Gibbs!' he shouted. But again there was no reply. 'Mrs Gibbs!' He let the door fall back in place and started to edge back towards the entrance. Something moved. Tom froze. Then whatever it was moved again and brushed against his leg.

Tom made a leap towards the entranceway and something leaped with him. He scrabbled up the step, hauling himself through, aware of some *thing* trying to squeeze between him and the light. Suddenly it made one huge effort and hurled itself past his arm and out, hurtling into the dunes beyond the track. It was a hare.

Tom collapsed, half in and half out of the barrow, his heart beating like a drum. Then he became aware of the laughter. It was Susannah Gibbs.

'Oh, Tom,' she said between breaths. 'Oh, Tom. Your face. You look as though you've seen the devil himself.'

'Why didn't you answer?' said Tom, climbing out and failing to see the joke.

'I was just having a little sport with you, Tom,' she said. 'Don't be cross with me. I couldn't bear that.' Her face seemed so full of concern for Tom's opinion of her that he found he could not hold a grudge against her and forced a laugh himself.

'Of course I'm not cross,' he said.

'I am glad to hear it,' said Susannah with a broad smile. 'But did I hear you say the bones of the old fellow are gone?'

'Yes.'

'Dear me,' she said with a little smirk. 'Abraham is not going to be pleased.'

'But who could have taken them?' said Tom.

'Perhaps old Redwulf walked out all by himself,' she said with a chuckle. Tom did not find this thought as amusing as Susannah seemed to.

'You do not seem very concerned,' he said.

'Oh, Tom,' said Susannah with a sigh. 'I try to be interested in Abraham's silly bones and rusty swords – I do, I really do – but I am afraid I rarely succeed.'

Tom dusted himself down and walked with Mrs Gibbs back towards the house. A barn owl floated moth-like over the creeks.

'Tell me about London, Tom,' said Mrs Gibbs. 'I want to know all about the latest fashions.'

'Well,' said Tom. 'I . . . I . . . I don't think I know much about that.'

Mrs Gibbs laughed. 'Oh, bother you men,' she

said. 'Surely you must know what colours the ladies are wearing this year. And what about my hair, Tom? I'm sure I will look every inch the country bumpkin when we go to London. People will stare.'

'I don't think people will stare,' said Tom. 'I mean, not for you looking like a bumpkin . . .'

Susannah Gibbs smiled. 'You are very gallant, Tom,' she said, hooking her arm through his.

'But are you are going to London?' Tom asked.

'I would not like to say until Abraham returns. I think it is intended as a surprise,' said Susannah Gibbs with a knowing smile. 'Perhaps we could all go to the theatre together? Do you go to the theatre, Tom?'

'Yes,' he said. 'Sometimes. Dr Harker took me to the opera last spring.'

'Oh, how marvellous! I would love to go to the opera. You must promise to take me when we come to London.'

'Yes,' said Tom. 'Of course . . .'

'I shall hold you to that, Tom Marlowe,' she said.

Just then, as they reached the back of the

house, Tom became aware of the approaching rumble of a carriage on the drive. He and Mrs Gibbs walked round to the front of the house to greet Mr Gibbs and the doctor as they returned from their expedition. Foley jumped down from the carriage and grabbed the bridle of one of the horses as it came to a halt. Dr Harker and Gibbs climbed out.

'Good afternoon, dear,' said Gibbs, kissing his wife on the cheek. 'I hope you have entertained our young guest.'

'Oh yes. I have had some sport at young Mr Marlowe's expense.'

Tom blushed a little and noticed Dr Harker raising an eyebrow.

'I hope Susannah has not taken advantage of your undoubted good nature, Tom,' said Gibbs. 'You must not let her tease you.'

'No, sir,' began Tom awkwardly. 'She has . . . I have . . . we have . . . that is to say . . .'

'Dear me,' said Gibbs. 'I can see that Susannah has led you a merry dance.'

'I am afraid we have some bad news for you, sir,' said Tom, eager to change the subject.

'Really?'

Tom told Gibbs about the missing bones, and just as his wife had predicted he was furious. He clenched his fists and snarled, then turned away, kicking out at a piece of wood lying on the ground and sending it flying into the air.

'Abraham,' said Susannah. 'Control yourself, please.' Gibbs turned angrily, opening his mouth as if to shout at her, but then checked himself and turned away. He stood for a while, his back to Tom and the others, head bowed, muttering and cursing at the empty creeks.

'Is there nothing we can do, Abraham?' asked Dr Harker gently.

'No,' said Gibbs forlornly. 'This is what I am up against, Josiah. Do you see?'

'But who would take the bones, Abraham? They have no real value to anyone but a student of history like yourself.'

'And yet they are gone,' hissed Gibbs. 'Who knows why? Maybe they were taken for sport or out of spite. Maybe they were hurled into the marsh to placate the ghost of Redwulf? The why does not matter, Josiah.'

'The why always matters, Abraham,' interrupted Dr Harker gently.

'I just want to understand the past, Josiah,' said Abraham, softening a little. 'Why can they not see the value in that?'

'They will,' said Dr Harker. 'I am sure of it.'

'But you see now my reasons for the business we conducted today?' Dr Harker nodded. 'I cannot stand idly by while my wife and I are besieged by ignorance.'

'So,' said Susannah Gibbs, 'you have completed your business, then? Am I to be told what it is?' Tom had the distinct impression that even while she asked this question, she felt sure she knew what the business was.

'Well, my dear,' said Gibbs, walking back and gently taking hold of one of his wife's hands. He had calmed himself but his face was still flushed. 'I know that you have been so greatly upset by all that has occurred here in recent weeks . . .'

'Oh you must not worry about me,' she said with a bright smile.

'But I do,' said Gibbs. 'I do. And this is something I had meant to do some time ago, but this resentment from the local populace over the burial mound has been the final straw . . .'

'Yes . . . ?' said Susannah.

'That is why I have signed over the bulk of my inheritance to the formation of a charitable foundation for the education of local children. We shall build a wonderful school here that will stand as a beacon of reason. It shall be called the Susannah Gibbs School. How about that? What do you say, Susannah?'

But Susannah Gibbs said nothing. She stood rooted to the spot initially, but then turned and ran as if blown by a sudden wind towards the house.

'Now then,' shouted Gibbs throwing up his hands. 'If there is a man in all England who can make the remotest claim to understanding womankind, then I should like to meet him, sir! I should like to meet him!' And with that, he too disappeared into the house.

8

FENRIR

Tom decided to go for a walk down to the beach the following morning. Mrs Gibbs had not appeared at breakfast and there had been an uncomfortable atmosphere in the house. Tom was only too happy to make himself scarce.

Small boats lay here and there on the mud of the creeks, stranded by the outgoing tide. Marsh birds scurried about, probing the dark silt with their beaks. A heron rose up lazily at his approach and flew off into the marshes with slow beats of its huge grey wings.

As Tom climbed to the top of the dunes, he immediately saw where Susannah Gibbs had disappeared to. There below him, she was riding her great black horse Raven at breakneck speed along the hard, rippled sand at the sea's edge.

Tom had never seen a horse run so fast, nor anyone ride with such reckless abandon. Raven's hooves thundered and even from a distance Tom could see his flanks glistening with sweat. Every now and again Susannah would let out a wild shriek, someway between exhilaration and rage, and urge her horse on.

Tom suddenly felt guilty for watching; as if he were spying on Susannah, and he turned away and descended the dunes. He felt a growing annoyance at Mr Gibbs, who seemed not to have any appreciation of his wife's feelings. Susannah Gibbs was clearly desperate to leave this desolate place and Tom, for one, could not blame her. Tom thought Gibbs seemed to think more about the locals and his precious artefacts than he did about his wife.

Tom had attempted to pass on some of these feelings to Dr Harker, but the doctor had told him that it was a foolhardy man indeed who attempted to open a window onto another man's marriage and Tom took the hint and said no more about it. Instead, as they walked, he told the doctor what Susannah Gibbs had told him of the legend.

'Hmm,' said Dr Harker. 'It does make you wonder why the barrow was not broken into before.'

'Sir?' said Tom.

'Before the knight-turned-hermit chose to guard it,' said Dr Harker. 'Who or what protected it in the centuries before that?' This had not occurred to Tom, but he had to admit that it was curious.

The lane was edged with hawthorns, some of which had grown to small trees, bent and hooked over by successive winter gales until they looked as purposefully designed as the yews in Gibbs's garden.

They passed an old man, hunched over like the hawthorns, carrying bundles of kindling. He had a clay pipe clenched between the only four teeth he seemed to possess. Dr Harker wished him 'Good day' and the old man nodded in reply without pausing.

After a while they came to a small round towered church. The lane ran along beneath the churchyard, so that one side of the lane formed its boundary wall. The wall was made of the same gingerbread-coloured stone as the garden wall of Low House, and likewise speckled with lichen and encrusted with all manner of tiny plants.

The turf of the graveyard overhung the wall and rose up in a soft mound, studded with grave-stones, the church sitting on top.

The tower of the church seemed to Tom more like the turret of a small castle, with a tiny window set into it high up with short fat little columns on either side capped with crude decorations. The whole building looked as though it might have been made of pastry.

'It is quite something, is it not?' said Dr Harker.

'It's beautiful,' said Tom. 'Not like Mr Wren's churches are beautiful, but beautiful all the same.'

'I agree,' said Dr Harker. 'London changes so quickly, Tom. I dare say they will have knocked St Paul's down in a hundred years time and built who knows what in its place. But here . . .' he said, 'time seems to run by a different clock. The ancient and the new living side by side.'

Looking through the railings into the churchyard, Tom and the doctor could see a new grave with a freshly carved headstone and they guessed it must be that of the servant, Margaret Dereham, whose death in the creeks had cast such a shadow over their arrival. Then Tom heard a strange noise approaching behind them and he turned to see what it was. Too late Tom saw that it was a gigantic hound galloping towards him.

He was knocked off his feet and thrown down onto his back. The massive hound pinned him to the ground, his paws on Tom's chest and his snarling face inches from Tom's own. The creature's fangs parted slightly as it prepared to lunge.

Dr Harker drew his sword and the hound switched his attention from Tom to the doctor. He growled and prepared to leap as a voice called out from some way down the path.

'Fenrir! To me!'

The hound's ears pricked up, it seemed to utter a disappointed groan and then loped off in the direction of the voice. Dr Harker sheathed his sword and helped Tom to his feet. As he did so, the hound reappeared at the side of a tall man dressed in black.

The man walked towards them and Tom now noticed he was holding a long black cane, its silver handle fashioned into the shape of a skull. He wore neither wig nor hat, and his long black hair hung about his shoulders, coiling and twisting in the breeze.

His face was handsome but almost as pale as the lace around his neck and Tom noticed that although his clothes were clearly made of the finest material, they were oddly old-fashioned, giving him the unsettling appearance of a ghost.

He wore black knee-length boots and a thick cloak hung around his shoulders, draping down to his calves like the folded wings of a crow. There was rich embroidery on his cuffs and on his waistcoat but it was all of black. Even the buttons of his waistcoat seemed to be fashioned of jet.

'What is the meaning of this? We are guests of Mr Abraham Gibbs,' said Dr Harker sharply. 'Who the devil are you? And I would thank you to keep a stronger control over your dog.'

'Had I not such a strong control over Fenrir,' said the man with a smile, 'your servant would be without a throat.'

'This is my assistant, Mr Marlowe,' said Dr Harker. 'You, sir, need some lessons in manners. And it will be your dog that will be missing its head if it attempts to attack my young friend again.'

'I think you may be underestimating Fenrir's speed,' said the stranger with a smile.

'And you are underestimating mine,' said Dr Harker. 'But if you doubt it, by all means set your creature to work.'

The stranger smiled again. 'There is part of me that is tempted to put this to the test,' he said. 'But I should be most upset to lose Fenrir if you prove to be the swordsman you claim to be, and I rather think you may. If you will allow me to apologize. My name is Lord Ickneld.' Tom remembered the man in the inn talking about the devil-worshipping lord. Dr Harker hesitated. 'Please. Fenrir knows everyone hereabouts. It is only your being strangers that seems to have provoked him. As he cannot do so himself, may I apologize on his behalf.' Tom looked at Fenrir, who was looking back at him and still growling under his breath, and thought the hound looked anything but apologetic.

'Very well. I am Dr Harker and this – as I have already said – is Mr Thomas Marlowe,' said the doctor curtly.

'Forgive me, gentlemen,' said Lord Ickneld. 'We are not used to strangers here. I hope you will not think badly of us.'

'Your apology is accepted, sir,' said Dr Harker. 'Now if you will excuse us, our hosts will be wondering what has become of us. Good day to you, sir.'

'Good day to you,' said Lord Ickneld.

Tom and Dr Harker nodded and turned away to walk back towards Low House. Tom had a great deal of trouble resisting the impulse to turn round. It was only the fear of seeing the hound Fenrir bolting towards him, or Lord Ickneld flapping his cloak and flying off like a raven that stopped him. But when they were about fifty yards down the track Lord Ickneld called after them and they both turned to look back.

'Beware, gentlemen!' he shouted. 'There is great danger here. Mortal danger!'

With that he turned, his cloak swirling round him, and strode away, his huge hound trotting alongside, finally disappearing from sight in a bend in the track.

9

BAMBERINI

The atmosphere in Low House seemed to have lightened a little by the time Tom and Dr Harker returned from their walk. Mr and Mrs Gibbs were at least in the same room, though they both looked relieved to have the distraction of Tom and the doctor's return.

'Ah,' said Gibbs, getting to his feet and coming out into the hall to greet them. 'How was your walk, gentlemen?'

'We had an interesting meeting with your neighbour,' said Dr Harker. Gibbs saw the mud on Tom's stockings and britches and the muddy paw prints on his chest.

'Lord Ickneld? He is responsible for this?' said Gibbs. 'He and that dreadful beast of his? Oh, this really is too much!'

'What a dreadful man he is,' said Susannah Gibbs, joining them. 'I wonder you haven't dealt with him, Abraham.'

'Dealt with him?' said Gibbs with a chuckle. 'And how am I to do that? He is a peer of the realm. His uncle is the sheriff.'

'Oh, Abraham!' Susannah sighed. 'I despair of you sometimes. There are times you need to forget about legal niceties and stand up for yourself. I don't think your precious Redwulf would have been so timid. Tom knows what I mean, don't you, Tom? He is learning to use a sword you know, is that not so, Tom?'

Tom shrugged, looking uncomfortably from husband to wife and then to Dr Harker. 'Yes . . . I . . . I must get changed out of these dirty clothes,' he said. 'I do not want to spoil your furniture. If you will excuse me.'

He went up to his room and changed into his only other set of clothes, feeling all the more like the printer's boy he had so recently been. When he was ready he returned to the others who were all now seated in front of the fire.

'Ah, Tom,' said Gibbs. 'I can only apologize for Lord Ickneld. The man is a law unto himself, I'm afraid.'

'It is not your fault, sir,' said Tom. 'In any event, Lord Ickneld apologized himself.' Both Susannah and Abraham Gibbs looked amazed.

'Apologized?' said Gibbs. 'You are honoured, Tom. Honoured, indeed.'

'Come and join us by the fire, Tom,' said Dr Harker. 'Mr and Mrs Gibbs were telling me all about Lord Ickneld.'

'Yes, Tom,' said Gibbs. 'He is rather a colourful fellow.' Susannah snorted. 'They say he even worships the devil.'

'And does he?' said Tom. 'Worship the devil?'

'Heaven only knows,' said Gibbs with a laugh. 'He has certainly had some rather strange parties at the hall. His guests are almost as peculiar as he is. There have been some rather astonishing stories . . .'

'Such as?' said Dr Harker.

Gibbs took a deep breath.

'Sacrifices,' he said.

'Sacrifices?' said Dr Harker with a wry smile. 'I trust you do not mean human.'

'No . . . I mean . . . Of course, it is nonsense,' said Gibbs. 'I believe he enjoys the scandal and fans the fires of these rumours himself by his eccentric behaviour. He is fiercely intelligent though.'

'Yes,' said Dr Harker. 'I got that impression. He is certainly intriguing. Do you have reason to see him often?'

'No,' said Gibbs. 'We meet at social events locally, but I'm afraid there is bad blood between us.'

'Really?' said Dr Harker. 'Why?'

'It's to do with the barrow actually,' said

Gibbs. 'Many years ago, the barrow was on Lord Ickneld's land. Lord Ickneld's father fell heavily into debt and was forced to sell the land. My father allowed him to keep Ickneld Hall and built Low House on the land. Without my father, Lord Ickneld would be penniless.'

'And the barrow?' asked Dr Harker.

'My father and Lord Ickneld's had a gentle-manly agreement that the barrow would be left untouched,' said Gibbs. 'But that was between them. I did not feel constrained by it and when the late Lord Ickneld passed away, I felt that I had a duty to see what it contained.' Dr Harker frowned. 'I see you disapprove, Josiah.'

'It is not for me to say,' said Dr Harker, 'but I take it that Lord Ickneld thinks the agreement should have been binding on you as it had been on your father.'

'Yes,' said Gibbs. 'And he is entitled to his opinion, of course. You have seen the way he dresses. He lives in the seventeenth century. I live in the eighteenth, Josiah, and proudly so.' Foley went round the table topping up glasses. Gibbs continued. 'I believe Ickneld deliberately adds credibility to these ridiculous stories of a guardian of the grave,' he said. 'It is well known that he believes in the world of spirits and goblins. Somehow it is far worse that a man of learning like that should encourage the ignorant in their superstitious babbling.'

At this moment Bamberini walked in, looking a little red in the face.

'Ah, Bamberini,' said Gibbs. 'Come and join us. We were talking about Lord Ickneld.'

'Lord Ickneld?' Bamberini looked slightly startled.

'Yes,' said Gibbs. 'Don't just stand there, man. Sit yourself down. Pour the fellow a brandy, Foley.'

'The very morning poor Margaret met her death,' said Susannah Gibbs, 'I bumped into Lord Ickneld on the back lane and he was frightfully rude and abusive.' Tom noticed that Bamberini stared hard at Mrs Gibbs and his face seemed to lose all of its colour.

'You have not mentioned this before,' said Gibbs.

'I know, dear,' she said. 'What with Margaret

and the funeral and such, it quite slipped my mind.'

'Do you see what we have to contend with, gentlemen?' said Gibbs, banging his fist into the table. 'Lord Ickneld is a law unto himself. But we are rational men, Josiah. We cannot be swayed by romance and hobgoblins. Let us find some other subject for conversation.'

They took the hint and the subject of Lord Ickneld gave way to others. Mrs Gibbs was as enthusiastic as always to hear about London and about Dr Harker's travels, and though Tom had heard many of the stories before, he was happy to hear them again.

Eventually, Bamberini begged their pardon and said that he must get back to work on the drawings and Gibbs went with him to the library. Mrs Gibbs said that she had some letters to write and left, leaving Tom and Dr Harker alone.

'Did you see Bamberini's face when Mrs Gibbs spoke of her argument with Lord Ickneld?' said Dr Harker.

'Yes, sir,' said Tom. 'What do you think it means?'

'I do not know. Maybe nothing at all. Shall we take a walk, Tom? Fresh air is always good for the thinking muscles!' Tom smiled and nodded, getting up from his chair.

As they left the garden gate, they saw Bamberini coming round the side of the house.

'Signor Bamberini,' said Dr Harker. 'I thought you were in the library hard at work.'

'*Si*,' said Bamberini. 'I am. I was. But I am not well in the stomach and I thought perhaps I would go for a walk.'

'I'm sorry to hear it,' said Dr Harker. 'Tom and I are likewise going for a walk. Perhaps some company might make you feel better.'

'No . . . No . . .' said Bamberini. 'I would rather . . . If you do not mind . . . I would rather be alone.' He looked as though he had intended to take the back lane, but changed his mind and headed along the track towards the dunes. 'Goodbye.'

A maid nearby was hanging washing on the line and tutted loudly. Tom and the doctor turned.

'Was there something you wished to say, my dear?' said Dr Harker.

'Beggin' your pardon, sir, it isn't none of my business to say,' said the maid.

'But if it was?' said Dr Harker. 'If it was your business to say?'

'The master won't hear of anything to do with the Sentinel, he won't,' said the maid, looking nervously about her.

'But we are not the master,' said Dr Harker, taking his purse from his pocket and shaking some coins into the palm of his hand.

'Well, sir,' she said, staring intently at the coins. 'It's the Beany-beany fellow there.'

'Signor Bamberini?' said Dr Harker.

'Him, yes,' she said. 'Oh, I know it ain't my place or nothing, sir,' she continued, looking round warily. 'But the foreign gentleman is always a-sneaking off to the Hall. I seen him do it, I have.'

'Are you sure?'

'Sure as I'm standing here, sir,' she said.

'And did you not think fit to tell anyone of this earlier?'

'I've just told you the master was insisting it was an accident and well, I couldn't see him taking kindly to me saying anything bad about his precious artist. Who was he going to believe? No, sir – I need this job.'

'So why say now?' said Dr Harker. 'How do you know I won't go straight to Mr Gibbs and say you have been spreading malicious gossip?'

'I don't know, sir,' said the maid. 'Sometimes a thing gets itself said whether you want it to or not, doesn't it sir?' She looked at the creeks. 'Besides, Margaret didn't deserve that. Nobody does.' She stepped a little closer and dropped her voice to a whisper. 'And I'll tell you something else while we are having this chat. He weren't in the house that day at all. The day that Margaret was killed.'

'Bamberini? How do you know?' said Dr Harker.

'I saw him with me own eyes, I did,' she said. 'He came walking down the lane and then he saw all the fuss there was over poor Margaret being pulled from the creek and he just came over as if he'd been there all the time. He looked as nervous as a lamb in a butcher shop and he had mud splattered up his stockings like he'd been in the creeks. Foreigners is all a bit suspicious if you ask me. No offence.'

'We are not foreigners,' said Dr Harker testily. 'We are from London.'

The maid shrugged. 'No offence,' she said, clearly unconvinced by the distinction. Her hand pecked the coins hungrily from Dr Harker's hand and dropped them in the pocket of her apron. 'Anyways, I must get on.'

Dr Harker and Tom walked away from the house until they were out of earshot of anyone there.

'I forgot to tell you, sir,' said Tom.

'What is that, Tom?'

'Mr Foley, sir,' said Tom. 'He lied about the bridle. Mrs Gibbs had no idea what I was talking about when I brought the subject up.'

'That is very interesting, is it not?'

'And what was Mr Bamberini up to, sir?'

'I do not know,' said Dr Harker. 'But he was as jittery as a kitten. We shall need to talk to him when he returns.'

But Bamberini did not return. He did not return for lunch and he did not return for dinner.

He had not returned when everyone had retired to bed. When Tom came down to breakfast with Dr Harker the following morning, Bamberini's place at the table was still vacant.

'Bamberini seems to have disappeared, Josiah,' said Gibbs. 'He can't be found anywhere. It's a most extraordinary thing.'

'Disappeared?' said Dr Harker.

'His bed has not been slept in.'

Tom and Dr Harker exchanged glances.

'Are his things still in his room?' asked the doctor. 'His paper, his drawings?'

'Yes,' said Gibbs. 'Why?'

'Because I fear that Bamberini must be in some trouble,' said Dr Harker. 'It seems unlikely he'd leave willingly without his work unless he was in a great hurry indeed. Vain and pompous though he may be, he is an artist to the marrow. It seems too much to hope that Bamberini's disappearance is unconnected with poor Margaret's death.'

Dr Harker asked if he might look in Bamberini's room and Gibbs agreed. Tom went with him and they were surprised to find how homely Bamberini's room was, with a vase of reeds on the windowsill and shells and stones he had collected from the beach.

A large piece of flint was acting as a paper-weight on a pile of drawings and Dr Harker picked them up and thumbed through them.

'He is a considerable talent, Tom,' said Dr Harker. 'Look at these drawings. Here is Low House . . . Here is St Felix's . . . Now look here – I wonder who this might be?'

'It is poor Margaret Dereham,' said Gibbs as he walked up behind them. 'Bamberini drew her a few days before her death.'

'But who is this, Abraham?'

'I cannot help you there, I am afraid,' said Gibbs. 'She is very striking. Maybe it is Bamberini's love back in Tuscany.'

'No,' said Dr Harker. 'I think not. It is dated 26th October 1716. It is someone he has met here.'

'Extraordinary,' said Gibbs. Mrs Gibbs called from downstairs, and he turned to leave. 'I am sorry, gentlemen. I must go.' He left them alone once more, Dr Harker still gazing into the eyes of the mystery woman. Tom picked up the drawing

of Margaret Dereham and turned it over. He saw
a word written on the back.

'What does this say, sir?' said Tom. Dr Harker
took the drawing and held it up, squinting.

'*Assassinata*,' he said. 'It says *assassinata*:
murdered.'

'You don't think it possible that Bamberini
killed Margaret Dereham?' said Tom.

'I do not know, Tom,' said Dr Harker. 'He is
irritable and arrogant, but I would never have
thought him capable of something like that.' He
sighed. 'Maybe there was an accident and
Bamberini panicked. We must let the local law
take its course, Tom,' he added. 'We must be
wary of seeming as though we Londoners know
best. My concern is only that Bamberini will
receive a fair trial given the prejudice he seems to
have encouraged with his constant criticism of
everything English.'

'He should be easy to catch at any rate,' said
Tom. 'There can be few answering to his
description in this area.'

'Yes,' said Dr Harker. 'But then if he really is a
murderer, he might already be aboard a ship.'

* * *

Later that morning, Dr Harker and Tom walked down to the beach. The doctor busied himself along the shore, picking up shells and pieces of flint, discarding some and pocketing others. Tom stood and watched the waves rolling in until a noise made him look behind him.

Above the dunes there were seagulls crying. There was something about their wild enthusiasm that caught his attention for they seemed to be hovering over the same spot like wasps above a windfall apple.

Tom climbed a steep bank of sand to see the focus of the gulls' interest, but his view was obscured by yet another dune. He climbed to the summit of that one and stood among the gently swaying grass stems and saw at once what was attracting them.

Bamberini's body.

10

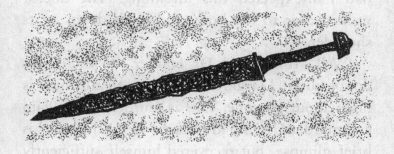

THE SEAX

'Dr Harker!' he shouted. 'Dr Harker!' And he then ran down the sand, waving his arms to drive away the gulls, which rose in a riot of resentful squawking, flying away to rest on nearby dune tops, waiting their turn to come back.

In his headlong rush to frighten the birds, Tom had given no thought to what he would find at the bottom of the dune, and he recoiled now from the grisly sight of Bamberini's corpse. As he turned away, Dr Harker appeared at the top of the dune and shook his head forlornly as if he had half-expected this all along. The doctor walked over to the body and knelt down at its shoulder.

'Well, Tom,' said Dr Harker. 'If there was doubt about Margaret Dereham's death there is none about this one. This is murder, Tom. Plain evil murder.' Tom had guessed as much from his brief glimpse, but recovered himself sufficiently to ask if the doctor had any idea how.

'He has been struck, Tom,' said Dr Harker. 'Struck with a huge force from above, on top of his head. Bamberini was not the tallest of men, but even so, I think we are looking for someone tall and very powerful indeed.'

Tom was keen to look elsewhere than at Dr Harker's examination of the body but as he looked about him a chill ran along his spine.

'Dr Harker, sir,' he cried. 'Look, sir. There are

no footprints in the sand! None save our own.'

Dr Harker looked around and nodded.

'Yes, Tom,' he said. 'You are absolutely right. And what do you think that tells us?'

'I . . . I . . . don't know, sir. That whoever killed Bamberini was not . . . that he did not . . . that he was a . . .'

'Ghost?' suggested Dr Harker with a grim smile. 'A ghoul? A phantom?'

Tom saw that he was being teased and blushed a little. 'I never said that, sir,' he said defensively.

'It tells us, Tom, that either the killer's prints have been erased by the wind . . .'

'The wind?'

'The wind, Tom,' said Dr Harker. 'Look about you. Even with this slight breeze, our prints will be vague by tomorrow and it was very windy last night. Or else, and I think this more likely, Bamberini was killed up on the dune top and rolled down. There is sand in the wound, do you see?'

Tom was happy to accept Dr Harker's word that there was.

'And the wind has erased the marks from his

rolling down.' he said. He blushed again, embarrassed by his eagerness to find a supernatural
explanation.

Dr Harker sighed, shook his head and asked
Tom if he would stay with the body while he
walked back to the house and told Gibbs. Tom
agreed and sat atop a nearby dune that afforded
no view at all of Bamberini's ruined features. He
frowned at the seagulls, who in their turn scowled
back at Tom.

After some minutes he could see a knot of
figures heading along the track from the house
towards him, and as they got nearer he could see
Dr Harker and Mr Gibbs at their head. Foley, he
learned, had been sent to fetch the sheriff.

Tom was surprised at how distraught
Abraham Gibbs was by the sight of Bamberini's
body. He slumped to the sand and held his head
in his hands. It was some time before he spoke
and then it was only with great difficulty.

'I am responsible,' he said finally, and Tom
looked at Dr Harker, taking it as an admission of
guilt.

Dr Harker gave Tom a withering look and

said, 'Of course you are not responsible, Abraham.'

'He was my guest, Josiah.'

'Whoever did this terrible thing is responsible, and he alone,' said Dr Harker. 'You must not blame yourself.'

Just then, Tom heard the distant sound of horses' hooves and turned towards the sound to see Foley and two other men riding towards them.

'Ah,' said Gibbs, standing up and trying to compose himself. 'Here is Foley with the sheriff.'

The sheriff dismounted with some difficulty and walked in the manner of a sailor walking the deck of a storm-tossed ship; hesitating now and then to balance himself and then setting off with renewed enthusiasm towards Gibbs.

The sheriff was in his forties, Tom surmised, and as thin as a pikestaff. His face was long, with a thin nose whose nostrils were permanently flared as if astonished by some unknown smell. His lips were rosy red and pursed, seemingly in sympathy with his surprised nostrils, while his chin was pushed back into his neck so that it hardly protruded at all. His wig was hastily applied and lopsided.

'Now then, sir,' he said. 'What do we have here?'

'Well, sir,' began Gibbs. 'My good friend Dr Harker here . . .'

'Dr Harcourt, eh?' said the sheriff. 'I knew a Harcourt once. Howwibly stout man. Large nose. Uncommon fine card-player though. The fingers of a small girl.'

'Dr Harker,' corrected the doctor, but the sheriff had already turned to Tom and had taken out a snuffbox.

'Who are you, lad?' he said, poking a pinch of snuff into his flared nostrils and taking a step back nervously. 'Not the culpwit, I hope. Should this lad not be in handcuffs? Woberts! Woberts! Bind this person immediately!' Tom could see that *Roberts* let a look of profound weariness cross his face for an instant, but did not move.

'No, sir,' said Tom holding out a hand, which only made the sheriff recoil further. 'I am Tom Marlowe, sir. I am Dr Harker's assistant.'

'They are both guests of mine, Gerald,' said Gibbs.

The sheriff eyed them warily and sniffed, closing his snuffbox with a loud click and putting it back in his pocket.

'Vewy well,' he said. 'If Abwaham here is vouching for you, that is enough for me. Dr Harcourt. Mister Marple. I am Gewald Fitzherbert, Shewiff.' Tom smiled and the sheriff squinted at him. 'What has occurred?' he went on. 'I am told that Gibbs's pet painter has been murdered. Is that cowwect?'

'Sadly it is,' said Dr Harker.

'He was foweign, don't you know,' Fitzherbert whispered conspiratorially to Dr Harker. 'Snuff?'

'Thank you, no,' said Dr Harker, backing away slightly.

'Do we know who done the dweadful deed?' asked the sheriff, turning to Gibbs.

'No, Gerald,' said Gibbs. 'The body has only just been found.'

'But do you know who done it?' he continued. Then he grinned mischievously and pointed at Gibbs. 'Did you do it, Abwaham? Eh?' he asked, nudging Gibbs in the belly with his elbow. 'Did you? Wouldn't blame you. Met him once. Insolent fellow.'

'I did not kill him, Gerald,' said Gibbs, looking increasingly embarrassed.

'You pwomise?' said the sheriff with a wink.

'I do.'

'Excellent!' said the sheriff. 'Then if you will all excuse me, gentlemen, I shall weturn to a wather fine meal I was hitherto in the enjoying therewof. Do you want Woberts to come for the body?'

'No, thank you,' said Gibbs. 'I shall pay for his burial, of course. It is the least I can do.'

'You are a soft-hearted soul, Abwaham,' said the sheriff. 'But as you wish. Farewell, Abwaham. Dr Harlot. Mr Marker.'

Fitzherbert walked off unsteadily towards his horse and gave them such an enthusiastic wave that he almost fell over and had to be helped into his saddle by Roberts, who looked at Tom and rolled his eyes before turning his horse and riding away with the sheriff.

'I apologise for Gerald,' said Gibbs. 'He has a

good heart, but sadly a very weak will when it comes to wine.'

'And will that be the extent of his interest in Bamberini's death then?' said Dr Harker. 'He did not even look at the body.'

'I am afraid that Gerald does not let the office of sheriff interfere with his social life,' said Gibbs. 'To be honest I was surprised to see him at all.'

Dr Harker shook his head, then knelt down beside the body once more and ran his hand over Bamberini's chest and neck. Tom, Gibbs and Foley stood over him.

'It is extraordinary,' he said. 'He seems to have been struck so hard that his neck was broken by the force of it.'

'But who could have done it?' said Gibbs.

'I don't know,' said the doctor. 'But he has been struck with enormous violence. It is hard to believe it is even the work of a human being.'

Tom stared at him and immediately thought of the giant figure he had seen his first night. He saw Foley lick his fleshy lips and look nervously at the creeks.

'You don't mean you are starting to believe these tales of the Sentinel I hope, Josiah?' said Gibbs.

'No, no,' said Dr Harker. 'Of course not. No – there must be an explanation. We are missing something; that is all. In any event, why would a guardian of the grave, supernatural ghoul or otherwise, attack Bamberini?'

'Maybe he was attacked by thieves?' said Tom and then with a flash of inspiration. 'Or by smugglers!' Again Foley licked his lips and looked away.

'Perhaps,' said Dr Harker. 'But here is his purse hanging from his waistcoat. It has not been touched. No, Tom, there is something else.'

'But if it was not a robbery as Tom suggests, then what?' said Gibbs. 'His being foreign seems to have annoyed many in the neighbourhood. But foreign and deeply irritating though Bamberini most certainly was, I cannot believe that anyone could have taken their annoyance with him to such extremes.'

'I don't know,' said Dr Harker. 'But whatever the cause, he did not deserve this, gentlemen. A stranger in a foreign land. It shames us that he should meet such an end in our country.'

'Hear, hear,' said Gibbs. 'Well said, Josiah.' Tom nodded. 'Foley,' Gibbs continued. 'Lend a hand and we'll put the poor fellow over the saddle of your horse and carry him back to the house.'

Foley and Gibbs lifted Bamberini's body between them and with a great deal of tugging and pulling managed to get the body across the saddle. Gibbs asked Tom if he might run back to the house and make sure Susannah was out of the way as the grisly sight of Bamberini would be too shocking for her. Tom was just setting off when he noticed something sticking out of Bamberini's coat pocket.

'Wait, sir,' he said, walking towards the body. 'What's that?'

'What have you seen?' asked Dr Harker.

'There, sir,' said Tom gingerly grabbing the object and pulling it out.

'Good Lord. It's a seax!' said Gibbs.

'What is it?' said Dr Harker.

'It is an Anglo-Saxon knife from the grave

hoard. It was one of the items I told you was stolen.'

All four men, even Gibbs, found themselves turning involuntarily, and with a curious dread, to look out across the dark expanse of the creeks.

11

THE GIANT

Tom went ahead to the house to ensure that Mrs Gibbs was kept occupied by the cook, so that they could bring Bamberini's body back without her seeing it, after which Tom was left to guard the hall against her reappearance while

Gibbs, Dr Harker and Foley carried the body down into the wine cellar.

While Tom was waiting for the men to come up from the cellar, the cook suddenly stepped out into the hall. Tom got ready to deliver a little pre-rehearsed speech to Mrs Gibbs involving several questions about her life in Bristol, during which he would lead her towards the dining room until the others had finished. But the cook was alone.

'Where is Mrs Gibbs?' he asked.

'She went out into the garden by the kitchen door,' said the cook. 'She'll be safely out of the way there.'

Then Tom heard a scream but could not tell in which direction it had come from. The cook put a hand to her chest.

'Lord save us,' she said. There was another and this time clearly from the marsh side of the house.

'It's Mrs Gibbs!' Tom cried.

He ran as fast as he could, skidding as he cornered the house. Beyond the garden wall he could make out a struggle. To his horror he realized that Susannah Gibbs was locked in the grip of a giant. She looked tiny against his bulk, like a doll in the hands of a sullen child.

'Hey!' called Tom running towards them. 'Stop!'

He paused to grab a log from the woodpile and ran on, shouting as bravely as he could. Suddenly Susannah was thrown to the ground and the giant made off. Tom was so enraged he began to chase him but Susannah called out.

'No, Tom,' she said. 'Let him go. I would not see you hurt and I am unharmed.'

'Are you sure?' said Tom, helping her to her feet.

'Quite sure,' she said. 'You were very brave just now.'

Tom blushed. 'But you are bleeding!' he said, noticing a trickle of blood running from a cut above her ear. 'We should get you into the house, Mrs Gibbs,' he added.

'Can I take your arm, Tom?' she asked. 'I do feel a little weak.'

Tom held out his arm and Susannah Gibbs took it, holding on more tightly than Tom had expected and leaning into him as they walked. He helped her into the house, feeling older than his years and more than a little proud. Foley was the first person they met.

'Madam?' he said, rushing forward. 'What's happened?'

'She was attacked,' said Tom. 'There was a huge man; a giant. I think it was the man I saw the night we first came.'

'A giant . . . ?' said Foley, looking shocked. 'A giant you say?'

'He had long hair,' said Tom, surprised by the question. 'A cloak of some sort, I think. Do you know him?'

'Come now, madam,' said Foley, ignoring Tom's question. 'I think we should get you inside and then I'll send young Patrick for the doctor.'

'I will be fine,' said Susannah Gibbs. 'Please don't fuss, Foley. I have Tom here to—' Susannah Gibbs fainted. Tom was caught by surprise and only just held her.

'Master!' called Foley, stepping forward to help Tom. 'Master! Come quick!'

'What the devil?' said Gibbs as he stepped into the hall and saw his wife unconscious, Tom holding her limp body and Foley whispering to her to revive her.

Gibbs strode over and took his wife from Tom, picking her up and carrying her towards the library. Susannah stirred, opening her eyes a little.

'Thank you, Tom,' she murmured over Gibbs's shoulder. 'My brave, brave Tom.'

Gibbs gently sat his wife down on a chair by the library door and then turned, his eyes ablaze with anger. 'Quickly, Tom,' he demanded. 'What happened?'

'Mrs Gibbs was attacked, sir,' said Tom. 'He was a big man. Very big.'

'I owe you a debt of thanks, Tom,' said Gibbs patting him on the shoulder. 'But we must talk later. The rogue may still be there. Dr Harker – will you come with me to search? If he is still around, I want him caught!'

'Of course,' said Dr Harker.

'Tom,' said Gibbs, unlocking the library door and helping his wife inside the room. 'Will you look after my wife? We don't know if the man was alone, Tom, so on no account must you leave Susannah alone.'

'Of course, Mr Gibbs,' said Tom.

'Good man. Foley,' said Gibbs, 'bring Tom a basin of water and some muslin for Mrs Gibbs's wound.'

'Really, my dear,' said Mrs Gibbs. 'I feel perfectly well. Take Tom with you. I do not need a nursemaid.'

'I am happy to stay,' Tom said.

'We have no time to debate this,' said Gibbs. 'Foley will guard the front door with a loaded pistol. Tom: here is the key; when we leave I want you to lock this door and do not unlock it until we return.'

'Yes, sir,' said Tom.

'Come, Dr Harker,' said Gibbs.

Gibbs and the doctor left the room, leaving Tom alone with Mrs Gibbs. After Foley had brought the basin and cloth as requested, Tom locked the door and helped Susannah to a chair by the fire. Then he dipped a piece of the muslin in the water and held it to the wound on her head. She winced a little but smiled, taking the cloth from him and holding it in place herself. Tom leaned down and put another log on the fire.

'You should keep warm,' he said. 'You have had a shock.'

'You are so kind, Tom,' said Mrs Gibbs. 'But really, I have had worse than this falling from my horse.'

'Yes,' said Tom with a smile. 'I saw you riding on the beach.'

'Did you? You did not say.'

'I thought it something private,' said Tom. 'A secret perhaps.'

Susannah Gibbs looked at him for a while and then smiled. 'You are an unusually perceptive young man,' she said.

'Not so unusual, I think,' said Tom. 'And not so very much younger than you.'

Mrs Gibbs looked away towards the fire. 'I wonder if they will catch him,' she said after a pause.

'I fear not,' said Tom. 'If he knows the marshes he will be long gone.'

'Tom,' said Mrs Gibbs, suddenly, 'could you fetch me some water from the kitchen? My throat suddenly feels as dry as the dunes.'

'I don't think I should leave you,' said Tom.

'Mr Gibbs is relying on me to stay with you at all times.'

'Oh for goodness sake!' she snapped, slapping the arms of her chair. 'I am not a child!' Neither spoke for a moment. The fire crackled and the wind whistled in the chimney. Susannah turned to face Tom. 'I apologise, Tom.'

'You have no need.'

'I've hurt your feelings.'

'My feelings don't matter,' he said, a little more sharply than he had intended.

'Of course they do, Tom,' she said. 'Of course they do. You are acting from the most noble of motives, but I will be quite all right.' Tom was about to make an objection when Mrs Gibbs interrupted him. 'Look, Tom,' she said. 'The key is in the lock there. Take it and lock me in when you leave, if that will make you feel better.'

'But Mr Gibbs—'

'Mr Gibbs is not here, Tom,' she said. 'Will you please do as I ask?' She smiled and dropped her voice to a whisper. 'Please, Tom.'

'Very well,' said Tom reluctantly. 'But I *shall* lock the door. We can't be sure there are not intruders. I shall be a moment, that is all.'

Tom unlocked the door and opened it, taking the key and putting it in his pocket. He took a last look at Susannah Gibbs but she was already looking into the fire. Tom locked the door behind him and walked briskly, almost running, to the kitchen where the evening meal was being prepared.

'Could I please have a glass of water for Mrs Gibbs?' he asked.

'What on earth has been going on?' said the cook. 'The master and the doctor and Mr Foley rushed out of here as if the world was coming to an end, grabbing muslin and suchlike . . .'

'Mrs Gibbs has been attacked,' said Tom. 'Just now, by the creekside. She has been hurt.'

'No!' said the cook, putting her hand to her cheek and leaving its imprint there in flour.

'I said no good would come of it,' said a maid.

'Hush now, Cathy,' said the cook. 'Mind to your own business and fetch Mr Marlowe here some more muslin. There's a roll of it in the pantry. Jane, you get him a glass of water on a tray, and here's a bowl, and I have some water on the boil. Cathy, will you go with him and see to Mrs Gibbs.'

'Yes, Mrs Tanner,' said the maid. 'But why ever didn't she just ring instead of sending the gentleman here? There's a bell-pull in the library.'

'Cathy,' said the cook, 'will you do as you are asked and keep your thoughts to yourself?'

'Yes, Mrs Tanner,' she said sullenly. 'Sorry, Mrs Tanner.'

'Young girls today,' said the cook to no one in particular, shaking her head and kneading a ball of dough with practised dexterity.

Tom followed the maid back into the hall. She carried a tray with a jug of cold water, a bowl of warm water, and a glass. Tom carried a length of muslin. Tom reached the door to the library first and taking the key from his pocket began to unlock it.

'You locked her in?' said the maid with a wry smile.

'At her own request,' said Tom. The maid continued to smile and Tom struggled to engage the key in the lock. Tom suddenly began to panic. Against Gibbs's express wishes, he had left Mrs

Gibbs alone. He began to dread what he might find.

After much fumbling, the door was opened and Mrs Gibbs was by the fire, quite the same as when he had left her.

'Thank you, Tom,' she said as he came in. 'As you see, I am quite well.'

'If you please, madam,' said the maid. 'I've brought some fresh water to bathe your wound.'

'It's only a scratch, I'm sure,' said Mrs Gibbs as Cathy the maid approached. Tom relocked the door.

'It's a nasty cut, madam,' said the maid. 'How did it happen?'

'Well, I do not really remember,' said Susannah. 'I was attacked by a huge figure by the marshes. He seems to have scratched me somehow.'

'What did the figure look like, miss?' said the maid. 'Was it the—?'

Suddenly there was a knocking at the library door and Tom, the maid and Mrs Gibbs all jumped with shock. Then they heard the voice of Mr Gibbs on the other side of the door and Tom quickly turned the key in the lock again. Abraham Gibbs strode in, followed by Dr Harker.

'Well, I've cleaned it as best I can,' said the maid hurriedly. 'If that'll be all.'

'Yes, Cathy,' said Mrs Gibbs. 'Thank you.' When the maid had left the room, Mrs Gibbs turned on her husband. 'You are trailing mud through the house. Oh, Abraham, really . . .'

'Confound it, Susannah,' he shouted. 'What has mud to do with anything? Look at you! It is an outrage!'

'It is a scratch,' said Susannah. 'Please calm yourself, Abraham.'

'This is how we are repaid,' said Mr Gibbs. 'This is how we are repaid for our benevolence!' Mrs Gibbs began to sob.

'Really, Abraham,' said Dr Harker. 'This is not helping matters. I think Mrs Gibbs should try and get some rest.'

Mr Gibbs looked at Dr Harker and then at his wife and the fury drained from his face.

'Dr Harker is right of course, my dear,' he said. 'There is nothing more to be done. We have checked the grounds but found no one. Foley is insisting on keeping watch by the door through the night.'

'Then go to bed,' said Dr Harker. 'Tom and I can make our own way up. Things never seem so grim by daylight.'

'Thank you,' said Mrs Gibbs. 'And thank you again, Tom.'

'Good night, Mrs Gibbs,' said Tom.

'Good night, gentlemen.'

12

THE EMPTY CHEST

It was the day of Bamberini's funeral. A strong
wind rattled the weather vane on St Felix's
tower and white clouds were being driven across
the sky like sheep across a hillside. The reeds
in the marshes whistled and hummed.

Tom, Dr Harker and Mr and Mrs Gibbs were the only mourners at the graveside. Gibbs had wanted his wife to stay back at Low House, but she had insisted on attending. Gibbs had worried that the funeral would be too upsetting for her, but Tom could see that she was made of stronger stuff than Gibbs gave her credit for.

When the funeral was over, they turned and walked towards the church gate and the back lane. Something made Tom turn round, and when he did so he saw Lord Ickneld standing over Bamberini's grave. Tom tapped Dr Harker on the arm and when the doctor turned, so did Gibbs.

'What is that fellow doing here?' hissed Gibbs and Susannah Gibbs turned to see what he was talking about.

'Listen,' she whispered. 'He is chanting some kind of spell over the body.'

Sure enough, Tom could hear Lord Ickneld reciting something by the grave, slowly and deliberately. The wind picked up again and swirled round the churchyard, causing Lord Ickneld's cloak to flap and flutter. More than ever he looked like a great crow about to take to the air.

He was too far away to make out the words and in any event, Tom was sure that Lord Ickneld was speaking in another language. Eventually, when he had finished, Lord Ickneld bowed to the grave, then turned and slowly walked away.

'Extraordinary,' said Gibbs.

'It's blasphemy, that's what it is,' said Susannah Gibbs.

'Come now, Mrs Gibbs,' said Dr Harker. 'We do not even know what he was saying.'

'Hmm,' she said dismissively. 'Whatever it is, you can be sure they are not Christian words.' And with that, she and her husband left the churchyard, leaving Tom and the doctor looking back towards the grave.

'Why would Lord Ickneld come to Bamberini's funeral?' said Tom.

'Why indeed, Tom?' said Dr Harker. 'Why indeed?'

They headed back to Low House. The wind was stronger than ever and blowing straight into their faces, making the walk back a struggle. Dr Harker had a hand firmly placed on his wig and they both leaned so far into the wind that had it dropped they should have fallen flat on their faces.

The bare branches of the hawthorns scratched and whispered. The last of the leaves still clinging to their twigs now lost their grip and took to the air like flocks of birds. Up ahead Tom could see Gibbs holding onto his wife as they battled against the wind. She looked so slight, it seemed to Tom that at any moment a gust might snatch her from Gibbs's grasp and whisk her away.

The smoke from the chimneys of Low House was almost horizontal by the time they reached the garden gate and an empty barrel was bouncing around the cobbles of the courtyard and crashing against the stable doors.

When they finally entered the house and closed the door behind them, Tom was amazed by the relative silence now that the wind was no longer roaring in their ears.

'Susannah is going to lie down for a few minutes,' said Gibbs as Dr Harker tried to rearrange his wig which had twisted round in the gale so that it half-concealed his face. 'Won't you warm yourselves with a brandy by the fire? I shall be with you presently.'

'Excellent,' said Dr Harker, picking hairs out of his mouth. 'After you, Tom.'

While Dr Harker warmed his hands at the fire-place, Tom walked across to the window and looked out over the marshes. The whole land-scape looked frantically alive; willows twisting and bending as if tugged by unseen ropes, reeds rippling and shivering and flattening themselves as if they would never stand straight again. Grey clouds raced by against a soot-black sky. Then suddenly Gibbs's voice rang out across the hallway.

'Dr Harker!'

Tom and the doctor ran to the sound of Gibbs's voice calling from the library. Tom ran in first to find their host standing over the treasure chest, looking into it in disbelief.

'What is it, Abraham?' said Dr Harker.

'See for yourself, Josiah.'

Tom and Dr Harker walked across to where Gibbs was standing and looked inside the chest.

'It's empty!' said Tom.

'What is it?' said Susannah Gibbs, appearing in the doorway. 'Are you all right, my dear?'

'Quite all right, Susannah,' said Gibbs. 'But the sword . . . everything . . . everything is gone!'

'How can it be?' said Susannah.

Dr Harker shook his head. 'Has anyone entered this room to your knowledge, Abraham?' he asked.

'No one has been in,' said Gibbs. 'As I told you before, the room has been kept locked since part of the hoard was stolen, and after Susannah was attacked, she and Tom were safely in here together. I unlocked the door myself to let them in, and gave the key to Tom when we left to carry out our search.'

'Yet someone *must* have gained entry,' said Dr Harker. 'What about the windows?'

'Impossible,' Gibbs said. 'As you know they are shuttered and barred. Even if someone had managed to get through both, the damage would be visible. Look about you. Nothing but the chest has been touched . . .'

'But how can you be sure that someone has not gained access to the library? Thieves can be skilful at opening locks. May not someone have made a copy of your key? Surely that must be the answer?'

Gibbs looked at Tom, then at Dr Harker and sucked air between his teeth. 'Very well,' he said. 'Secrecy is pointless now. And keeping it from you suggests I do not trust you . . .'

'Yes?' said Dr Harker.

'Well,' said Gibbs. 'After the item was found on Margaret, I took to taking a precaution when I shut the hoard away; I placed a small hair from my wig into the lock of the library door. It was too small to notice and any tampering with the lock would have dislodged it. The door had not been touched.'

'Bravo,' said Dr Harker. 'You have your father's ingenuity. But nevertheless, a theft has taken place. We simply do not know how.'

Suddenly there was a loud crash and Tom turned to see one of the tall vases that stood either side of the window had fallen and smashed.

'Oh bother!' said Susannah. 'They were a wedding gift from my Aunt Augusta. I am such a clumsy oaf!' She began to sob. 'Sorry,

Abraham. Here I am sobbing over a silly vase while you have lost all your treasured grave goods.'

Gibbs did not reply. He simply stood staring into the empty chest. Eventually Dr Harker suggested they all go and sit down and Susannah asked a maid to bring some tea. Tom remained in the library, trying and failing to explain the disappearance of the hoard.

Then, out of the corner of his eye, Tom saw Foley walking down the garden path, nervously glancing about him. When he got to the gate he opened it, looked once back at the house – making Tom duck behind the shutters – and set off towards the church and the rest of the village.

Tom went outside as quickly and as quietly as he could. The air was cold and damp and the sea fret that been drifting in all morning was thickening. He left the garden and headed the same way as Foley.

Within yards, the mist had thickened to such a pitch that the lane was visible only in bursts as the mist occasionally thinned to allow something like normal vision. But even when the mists parted, Tom could see no sign of Foley ahead of him and stopped, realizing that this pursuit was pointless. He was just turning to head back to the house when, through a gap in the creekside hedge, he saw a movement in the marshes.

Tom left the track and peered into the mist. There it was again. Tom was sure it was Foley and looking carefully ahead of him, he decided to take some careful steps out into the marsh. After all, he thought, if Foley could find his way across, he certainly could.

It was only when he had hopped several hummocks into the creeks and the mist had swirled about him cutting off all view of the track and the village beyond that it occurred to him with sickening suddenness that the figure he had seen might not be Foley at all. And now he had no idea how to find his way back through the creeks.

13

THE FIGURE IN THE MIST

There could be no mistake this time. Appearing some yards off and then disappearing into the mist once more was a figure – and it was certainly not Foley. The man, if man he was, wore no hat, and Tom could just make out his long hair falling lankly about his shoulders. Other than that, he was as featureless as a shadow.

Tom's impulse was to run. But run where? He had no idea what direction the house lay in, even if the ground had been solid. And then it occurred to him that the figure might be Lord Ickneld. He did not wear a hat. He had long hair. He would undoubtedly know the marshes.

Tom had no wish to meet him again, but the thought of such a simple explanation for the stranger's identity gave Tom heart. So, instead of fleeing he called out, weakly at first, but then more loudly.

'Hallo!' he shouted. 'Hallo there!' The act of calling out calmed him a little. In calling to the mysterious figure, Tom felt as though he were making it seem more human. He was lost and calling to a stranger for help, that was all. But there was no reply.

Tom raised both his hands to his face to call out again and took half a step forward. A rabbit that had been crouching in a patch of heather at Tom's feet lost its nerve and bolted away. The sudden movement made Tom lurch backwards and he lost his footing, sliding down the greasy hummock and into the mud of the creek.

Panic overwhelmed him instantly. He grasped wildly at the heather and grass in front of him, but they could not bear his weight and simply came away in his hands. Within seconds he was calf-deep in mud.

Tom called out again, desperately this time. He tried to pull one of his feet out, but this only made matters worse as he lost his balance and fell sideways into the mire. He floundered wildly and managed to get himself upright once more. But now he was waist-deep in the mud and sinking fast.

'Please!' he called. 'Is there anyone there? Help me please! I'm sinking! Dr Harker! Anyone!'

No reply came but a mocking birdcall and even that sounded miles away. The mud was at his chest and felt chill against his pounding heart. The lower part of his body was gripped as if by a mighty fist with a grip as cold and hard as Death's.

Tom looked about him as the mud slipped around his throat. Only his arms and head now lay above the mud. Soon he would slip below the surface and be sucked down into its depths. He closed his eyes in a rage against his fate.

When he opened them he saw a shape materializing out of the swirling mist, moving swiftly towards him and taking human form as it did so. The phantom became more and more distinct, though no less fearsome, as the man who now stood above Tom was the giant who had attacked Susannah Gibbs.

He held a great staff in one hand and wore a long dark woollen cape. The staff, his long hair and gigantic appearance gave him the look of St Christopher, albeit a rather terrifying St Christopher. So unnerving was he, in fact, that when he crouched down and held his staff out toward Tom, he did not at first move.

The giant growled and frowned, pushing his staff towards him. Tom felt himself sink a little further in the oozing mud and did not hesitate again. The man grabbed and hauled at Tom so that he thought his arms might be pulled from their sockets, but the giant did eventually succeed in pulling him free.

They both collapsed onto solid ground, Tom gasping from relief and his rescuer from exhaustion. Tom wondered at how close he had come to death; it had clearly taken all the strength of even a giant like this to free him. He cast a shivering glance back down towards the mud.

'Thank you,' he said. 'You saved my—'

The giant stood up and looked up into the sky, clenching his fists as he did so.

'You saved my life!' Tom said again. But by now his relief at being freed from the mud had been entirely erased by this new fear of the stranger in front of him.

The giant snorted derisively and then he strode towards Tom who flinched at the blow he felt sure was coming, but the man walked straight past him. After a few yards, he turned and grunted at Tom, waving with his hand and indicating he was to follow.

In no time at all they were at the wall of the house. Tom was amazed at how close he had been. Without a word, the giant turned and walked away into the marsh, the mist gradually erasing his form until there was no trace.

Tom staggered back to the house. His legs suddenly began to feel like lead. Dr Harker was standing at the garden gate looking out to sea when he saw Tom approaching.

'Tom!' he shouted. 'Whatever has happened, lad?'

'I slipped in the creeks, sir . . . I was following someone – Foley – but it wasn't him, sir . . . It was someone else . . .'

'It's all right, Tom,' said Dr Harker. 'Put your arm round me and I'll get you inside.'

'But I'm covered in mud, sir,' said Tom. 'Your clothes will be ruined . . .'

'Put your arm round me, Tom, before you fall.'

Dr Harker took Tom into the house and Tom was surprised to see Foley suddenly appear at his side, looking a little flushed.

'Is everything all right, gentlemen?' he enquired and then saw the mud. 'Dear heaven!'

'Mr Marlowe has had a fall in the creek,' said Dr Harker.

'You're a lucky man then, sir,' said Foley. 'Most people only slip the once.'

'I was rescued,' said Tom. 'By the stranger who attacked Mrs Gibbs.'

Foley frowned and licked his fish-like lips. 'If you would like to follow me, sir,' he said, 'you should get yourself out of those clothes or the cold might finish what the creek started.'

Tom followed Foley up the stairs with Dr Harker behind him.

'Do you have another suit of clothes, sir?' Foley asked.

'I'm wearing it,' said Tom forlornly. 'I had changed after my last tumble with Lord Ickneld's hellhound.'

'Goodness, Tom,' said Susannah Gibbs, opening the library door and stepping out into the hall, a wicker basket over one arm. 'Whatever has happened?'

'I . . . I . . . fell' said Tom. 'I slipped and fell in the marshes.'

Mrs Gibbs looked pale and put a hand to her mouth. 'Tom!' she said. 'You could have been killed.'

'I know,' he said 'I was—'

'Lucky,' interrupted Dr Harker. 'No more

chatter now. You will catch your death, Tom.'

'Dr Harker is right, Tom,' said Susannah. 'You cannot stand here talking with these wet clothes on. You will catch a terrible chill. Foley, get Mrs Tanner to heat some water and Tom can have a hot bath.'

'But I have no clothes to change into,' said Tom.

Susannah Gibbs smiled. 'Such problems are easily solved,' she said. 'Let me just finish clearing up in here first. I am trying to see if I can mend Aunt Augusta's vase, you see. I want to pick up the pieces before Cathy comes in and throws it all away. I know it does not rate very high in importance next to rusty old swords and the like, but I was fond of it. Now off with you, Tom; you are actually starting to smell like the marsh.'

Dr Harker smiled. Tom scowled. He had only just cheated death and was not ready to be teased.

He went to his room and began to take off his muddy clothes. Foley arrived carrying a tin bath, which he placed in front of the fire, behind a screen. After a nervous nod in Tom's direction he left, only to reappear a little later with some hot water. As Tom sank into his bath, there was a knock on the door.

'Yes?'

'It's only me,' said Susannah Gibbs, walking in holding some clothes under her arm. Tom was seized by a panic that she might walk round the screen, but she seemed to sense this and called out.

'I have brought you some clothes, that is all. I shall put them on the bed.'

'Thank you,' said Tom, relaxing. 'Did you find all the pieces of the vase?'

'The vase?' said Mrs Gibbs. 'Oh, yes . . . thank you. I hope you are scrubbing well, Tom,' she added, suddenly peeping over the screen. Tom jumped, splashing water and almost tipping the whole bath over. Mrs Gibbs left his room laughing to herself, and after a moment Tom began laughing himself.

Tom joined Dr Harker and his hosts some time later as they drank tea in front of the window.

'My word!' said Dr Harker as he walked in. Tom was wearing a black suit with a dark-green silk waistcoat embroidered with intricate designs shot through with gold thread. There was a bunch of lace at his throat and more on his cuffs.

'These clothes are too fine for me,' said Tom.

'Nonsense, Tom,' said Mrs Gibbs. 'You look splendid, does he not, Dr Harker.'

'I must say that he cuts a very fine figure indeed,' the doctor replied.

'I bought these clothes for Abraham on our last trip to London,' said Mrs Gibbs with a sigh. 'But of course he never wears them.'

'When do I ever get the chance, my dear?' said Gibbs. 'They are too fine for working or walking and I would look a peacock among the gentlemen hereabouts.'

'And you would rather look a partridge,' said Mrs Gibbs. 'I know very well.'

'There is nothing wrong with partridges,' said Gibbs. 'Everything has its place.'

Mrs Gibbs clenched her fists. 'You do so vex me when you talk like this,' she said. She turned to Tom and smiled. 'You look very fine, Tom. It makes me happy to see them worn.' With that she left the room.

'I hope I have not caused any trouble between you,' said Tom.

'No, no,' laughed Gibbs. 'Susannah is determined to make a fashionable gentleman of me, but she is going to fail. She is as stubborn as a stone wall sometimes, but her tempers pass as quickly as they arrive. It is one of the many reasons why I love her so. Susannah would rather we moved to London. She craves society.'

'One can hardly blame her for that,' said Dr Harker. 'She is young.'

'I know,' said Gibbs. 'But there is society of a sort here. She will learn to love it here, I know she shall. And when we have the school here, Josiah, and Susannah is involved with that, then she will forget all about opera and silly things.'

'I am sure you are right,' said Dr Harker, in a voice Tom had come to know as usually expressing the opposite of the words spoken.

14

FOLEY

As soon as Tom could be alone with Dr
Harker he told him how he had been following Foley when he had become lost in the marshes
and how he was sure that the giant who had
attacked Mrs Gibbs and saved him from the creek

was also the figure he had seen from his window on their first night at Low House.

If it was, then someone in the house knew the giant because Tom had heard them whispering. Tom wondered if that person might be Foley.

'Well done, Tom,' said Dr Harker. 'I believe we might be getting somewhere finally. We need to talk to Mr Foley, I think.'

Tom and the doctor found Foley in the court-yard attempting to fix a faulty handle on Gibbs's coach. Dr Harker told him that they needed to speak to him and Foley ushered them into the relative privacy of a barn.

'I think you know more than you are saying about the recent events at this house, Mr Foley,' said Dr Harker.

'I'm sure I don't know what you mean,' said Foley nervously.

'Come, man,' said Dr Harker. 'We are not fools. What do you know of the giant who attacked Mrs Gibbs and who pulled Tom from the creek?'

Foley looked away and licked his lips. 'His name is Matthew,' he said finally. 'He was

Margaret's sweetheart.' Tom looked at him in amazement. 'God's honest truth. They were to be wed. She loved him and he loved her like I never saw a man love anything. Matthew's a mute, sir. He can only make grunts and the like and because of it people make the mistake of thinking he's simple. But he isn't. Not by a long way. Margaret saw it straightaway and he loved her for it.'

'But why keep this a secret?' said Dr Harker. 'Why have you not mentioned this to Mr Gibbs?'

'See how it looks, sir,' said Foley. 'They're already saying Margaret was a thief. What do you think they'd say if I told them about Matthew, who as it happens keeps ill company even though he's a good lad at heart? What with him being so big and the like, if I told them she'd been killed, they might think it was him, though he would never have harmed a hair on her head.'

'He tried to kill Mrs Gibbs,' said Tom.

'If Matthew had tried to kill Mrs Gibbs,' said Foley, 'then she'd be dead, sir. You can count on that. Matthew could snap a tree in two if he was of a mind to. And have you forgotten how he saved your life?'

'I saw him attack Mrs Gibbs,' insisted Tom. 'She was lucky to come away with a cut to her head.'

Foley licked his lips and frowned. 'I can't say you never saw what you say you saw, and it ain't my place to say you might be mistaken, sir, but all it don't figure. Not Matthew. He was hoping to move away. Him and Margaret were thinking of making a new life somewhere else. Margaret had some family in the Americas and they thought they might go there. Accuse him if you like. Him being mute, sir, how could he say it was otherwise?'

Tom had the impression he was being called a liar and opened his mouth to speak, but Dr Harker interrupted first.

'Why do you think Margaret was killed and did not just slip and fall?'

'Margaret knew those creeks like the back of her hand,' said Foley. 'I never believed she just fell. Besides, we did a lot of pushing and pulling to get her out, and first off I thought it might be that—'

'What?'

'The bang she'd taken to the back of the head,' said Foley. 'But it weren't us, sir. She already had that when we brought her out. No, sir, I believe she was killed. I tried to tell Mr Gibbs, but he wouldn't listen. He just thought I was talking about the Sentinel, but I wasn't.' He leaned forward conspiratorially. 'The village folk think she was killed by the Sentinel because of the bracelet they found on her, but I'll tell you something; she never had that bracelet on when we pulled her out, I'd swear on the Bible.'

'You mean someone put it on later?' said Dr Harker.

'I don't accuse no one,' said Foley. 'Although the foreign gentleman, sir, he was forever going to and fro along the back lane; and he was up to something the day Margaret was killed.'

'We heard that he appeared with muddy stockings.'

'Yes, he did, sir. And what with him having access to the stuff from the barrow . . .'

'And have you passed these suspicions on to anyone else?'

'Me, sir?' said Foley. 'Why would I do that? Who would I . . . ?'

'Have you for instance passed them on to Matthew?'

Foley looked at the floor.

'Bamberini was killed by someone wielding great force,' said Dr Harker. 'The kind of man who could break a tree in two.' Foley licked his lips again. 'Did you pass on your suspicions about Bamberini to this Matthew?'

'I . . . I . . . I don't know,' said Foley. 'I may have said something of the sort.'

'If it turns out that this man killed Bamberini because of something you might have said, you will bear some of the responsibility for it!' said Dr Harker. 'And what were you up to when Tom followed you in the back lane?'

'I was hoping to see Matthew if you must know,' said Foley defensively. 'I was going to warn him not to do anything rash. He's been watching the house as you know, but he wasn't there.'

'Listen well,' said Dr Harker forcefully. 'Bamberini was a guest in this land and I intend to find his killer even if no one else seems in the slightest degree concerned!'

Foley was taken aback by the vehemence of Dr Harker's outburst. So was Tom. Dr Harker leaned forward until his face was only inches away from Foley's.

'Either you tell me now where I might find this Matthew,' he said, 'or I will see to it that at the very least you lose your place of trust in this house, though I think we already have enough for me to prosecute you myself as an accomplice to murder!'

'I will not help you,' said Foley through gritted teeth. 'I shall find another position if needs be. And I'll take my chances with any prosecution too for that matter. Better that than what'll happen to me if it gets about that I peached. Hanging looks pretty beside that, gentlemen, take my word.'

'Who are you frightened of? Matthew? I thought you said he was no killer.' Foley made no reply. 'Very well then,' Dr Harker concluded with a sigh. 'As you wish.'

Foley looked suspicious. 'You no longer desire my help?' he said.

'I can hardly force you to help now, can I?'

'No you can't,' said Foley. 'If that is all, then I'll bid you good day, sir.'

'But what I can do,' said Dr Harker, 'is let it be known that you *did* help me.'

Foley stopped in his tracks. 'Do you realize what that would mean, sir?' he said.

'I do indeed,' said Dr Harker. 'It is a step I would not want to take, but it seems you give me no choice. If you help me, I will do all in my power to prevent your help being revealed. But if you do not help, then I will do everything in my power to see that the lie of your helping me is spread as far and wide as is humanly possible.'

'You—' Foley turned as if he intended to strike Dr Harker, but quickly thought the better of it. He was trapped and he knew it. Slowly and sullenly he sat down on a barrel, head in hands.

'Finding Matthew might not bring you good health,' he said. 'But as you're determined to know, then you could do worse than try the Cursing Pedlar in Dornham.' He smiled. 'And I wish you luck, sir.'

15

THE CURSING PEDLAR

Tom and Dr Harker set out for Dornham.
They followed Foley's instructions and
travelled by a green lane that took them over the
brow of a hill. Between the stems and branches of
the bare hedges, they caught glimpses of the sea

and the sunlight glinting on the weathercock on St Felix's church.

The walk was a pleasant one and Tom almost began to forget the purpose of their journey, so caught up was he in the unusual sights and sounds of the landscape about him. Until, that was, Dr Harker stopped in his tracks and turned to him with a grave expression. They were just at the outskirts of the village.

'Tom,' said Dr Harker. 'Once again, we find ourselves drifting into fog. We do not know what lies ahead in the Cursing Pedlar. We need to have our wits about us.' He smiled. 'Stay close by, Tom. There's no one I'd rather have at my side.' Tom smiled back.

Entering the village, Tom followed the doctor into the inn. There were a number of tables set about on a filthy plank floor. The walls were wood-panelled and the ceiling low and stained brown with pipe smoke. The windows were small and it took Tom a few seconds to adjust his eyes to the gloom. They walked to the bar.

'We don't often have call to serve gentlemen

such as yourselves, sirs,' said the innkeeper. 'Do you need a room?'

'No thank you,' said Dr Harker. 'We have no need of a room.'

'But you are not from hereabouts? Not that I'm curious at all. I have no curiosity. None whatsoever.'

'No, we are from London,' said Dr Harker.

'London, eh?' said the innkeeper. 'I couldn't see myself living in a place like that.'

'You've been there?'

'Me, sir? London, sir? No, sir. I haven't been further than Lynn my whole life.'

'You have no urge to see the world?'

'I have no curiosity you see, sir, as I just told you,' said the innkeeper. 'None at all. It's never interested me what's over the brow of some hill or other. I say let the people over the hill look at what's there and I'll look at what's mine. Now if you don't need a room, you must be staying somewhere local, gentlemen.'

'Yes,' said Tom. 'We are guests of Mr Gibbs at Low House.' He detected a momentary change in the atmosphere, as if all the customers in the inn had flinched at his words. The innkeeper certainly paused before answering.

'Low House?' he said. 'It's become a dangerous place of late, has it not gentlemen? Were you there when poor Margaret Dereham was killed?'

'Killed?' said Dr Harker.

'Met her death, I meant to say,' said the innkeeper. 'It's a terrible business.'

'Yes,' said Dr Harker.

'And there was some Spaniard he had working for him killed too, they say,' said the innkeeper. 'Though I'm sure it's no business of mine.'

'Italian,' said Tom.

'Beg pardon, sir?'

'Bamberini,' said Tom. 'The man who was killed. He was Italian. From Tuscany. He was a Tuscan.'

'Whatever he called himself, he had no business being here,' said the innkeeper matter-of-factly. 'Though I'd not see him killed, rest his soul, foreign or not.'

'That's very Christian of you,' said Dr Harker coldly.

The innkeeper caught the doctor's tone and

frowned. 'What is it that I can do for you gentlemen?' he asked.

'We are looking for a man you may know.'

'I *may* know him, sir,' said the innkeeper. 'And I may not. As I told you . . .'

'Yes, yes,' interrupted Dr Harker. 'You have no curiosity.'

'None at all.'

'Well I do,' said Dr Harker forcefully. The customers dropped all pretence at not listening and turned to face them. 'We are looking for a man – a big man – who knows the marshes.'

'And why's that?' asked a man at a nearby table.

'He saved my friend here from drowning in the creek and we wish to reward him,' said Dr Harker.

'Is that so?' said the man, picking up a club and tapping it against the palm of his other hand with a crooked smile. 'Give me the reward and I'll see he gets it.'

'I think not,' said Dr Harker, drawing his sword. The man got to his feet, the chair scraping backwards on the tiled floor with a piercing shriek.

'Jacob!' said the innkeeper. 'We don't want no trouble.'

Two other men rose to stand by him. Tom saw a movement out of the corner of his eye and saw another man move across to block his and the doctor's exit. The innkeeper took out a cudgel and placed it in front of him on the bar. The man at the door smiled and drew a sword.

'Remember our lesson, Tom,' said Dr Harker.

Tom snatched the cudgel from the counter and edged forward, inviting the man to attack, which he did, lunging forward at Tom's chest. Tom side-stepped the sword, grabbed the man's cuff, and brought the cudgel round with a sharp crack to the side of the man's head. He dropped like a sack of flour.

'Well done, Tom!' said Dr Harker.

Tom quickly took the unconscious man's sword, turning to join Dr Harker against the three men, who now seemed less keen to engage in combat. Pride made them brave however and the man who had first spoken leaped at Dr Harker with a club.

The doctor chopped the club in half, lunging

forward and punching the hilt of his sword into their attacker's jaw. The man lurched backwards, knocking one of his comrades over the table.

The third man pulled a knife but Dr Harker struck at his forearm making him howl in pain and drop the knife on the floor. The first man jumped back to his feet but Dr Harker put the point of his sword against his throat.

'If I had wished it,' he said, 'that man would have no hand and I would be pulling this blade from your heart. Say the word and that can still be the case.'

The man's eye twitched and the muscles of his face tensed and flickered.

'Very well,' he said finally. 'Put down your sword. There's none shall harm you. You have my word.' After a moment's hesitation, Dr Harker put down his sword and the man backed off, rubbing his throat. He nodded towards the door and the man there moved, opened it and left.

'You are quick with a sword, friend,' said the man.

'As quick as I need to be for an old man,' said

Dr Harker. The man laughed. 'Now do you know this man we seek?'

'Aye,' he said. 'I know him. Come on, I'll take you to him.'

Dr Harker eyed him suspiciously. 'Why the change of heart?'

'You bested me fair and square,' the man said. 'I took you for some London windbag, but you proved me wrong. You must let me make amends. Come with me now and I'll take you to the man you seek, I swear it.'

'Very well then,' said the doctor. 'Lead on.'

The man smiled and walked past them towards the door. Dr Harker followed and Tom joined him, feeling the gaze of the innkeeper burying in his back.

'Keep your wits about you, Tom,' said Dr Harker as they stepped into the daylight.

'Good advice,' said a voice beside them, followed by the clicks of several pistols being cocked.

'So this is all your word is worth,' said Dr Harker as his sword was taken from him.

The man walked back towards them.

'I swore no harm will come to you, and none shall, much as I am tempted to repay you for that blow to my jaw.'

'Then what is the meaning of this?' said Dr Harker.

'It is necessary is all I can say,' said the man. 'You shall have to trust me.'

'Do we have any choice in the matter?'

'None,' said the man and with a nod from him, hoods were put over Tom's and the doctor's heads. 'This is for secrecy only,' said the man. 'If I wanted you dead, you'd be meat, be sure of that.'

'Well, come on,' said Dr Harker. 'Or we shall die of boredom.'

The man laughed. 'You have some spirit, friend, I'll grant you that.'

Tom and the doctor were led away and made to climb onto what turned out to be a cart. Some kind of cloth was laid over them as they were made to lie down and the cart moved off.

The journey was extremely uncomfortable. Even through his hood, Tom could feel his head banging against the head of a nail with each stone or rut the cartwheels rattled over. They were both very grateful when the cart came to a halt and they were helped out and led a few yards to have their hoods removed.

Tom looked about him to discover that they were in a barn. Huge wooden beams, wider than a man's body, rose up and arched over them, knitting themselves together over their heads. In front of them were seven men, all of whom had black cloths tied across their faces, hiding all their features below the eyes.

16

SEVEN MASKED MEN

Tom felt a bead of sweat run down his throat. Despite the disguises, Tom could see that none of these men were the man who had helped him from the creek and attacked Susannah Gibbs.

'You said you could take us to the man we seek,' said Dr Harker.

'First we need to know what you want with him?' asked one of the masked men.

'I told you in the inn,' he said. 'I wanted to reward him.'

The man took his mask off and smiled at them. A bruise was already beginning to show on his jaw. 'You have a good memory for voices,' he said. 'That isn't such a healthy gift to have. And I don't believe you about this reward. Not after this attack on Mrs Gibbs now.'

'You know about that?'

'Servants are all gossips,' he said. 'So what's your real business with him?'

Dr Harker sighed. 'Very well,' he said. 'The truth is that we think he may know something of the murder of Margaret Dereham.'

'You think him a murderer now?' said the man. 'One minute you want him rewarded, the next you want him hanged. You're not making me too eager to tell you his whereabouts.' Dr Harker said nothing. 'And you, lad?' continued the man. 'You think a man who'd risk his own life pulling you from the marshes is the sort to commit murder?'

'No,' said Tom and all of a sudden he was certain of it. 'I don't think he is. But all the same he did attack Mrs Gibbs.'

'I know the man of what we speak,' said the man. 'He'd no more take to the air than kill that harmless girl. A girl he loved. As for attacking Mrs Gibbs, I can't say.'

'I see,' said Dr Harker. 'But then why has he been watching the house?'

'Because he knowed Margaret was murdered,' said the man. 'I told him to stay away but he can't keep away and who can blame him. Someone in that house killed his beloved.'

'And did he think it was Bamberini? Did he think it was the foreign painter?' asked Dr Harker.

'He didn't kill him, if that's what you're meaning,' said the man. 'Matthew was here with me attending to some importation business if you catch my meaning.'

'And you would swear to that?' said Dr Harker.

'I don't think my word would help,' he said. 'If

we are talking a court of law. But here and now, I do swear it and you may be assured that rogue as I am, I do not swear lightly. I for one won't grieve for the foreigner if he killed Margaret. But Matthew had naught to do with his murder. We had heard that the foreigner might be to blame, but he was dead before Matthew left here, and I'll swear on a hot iron to it.'

Just then, a door opened behind the seven men and the giant Matthew walked in. The man from the inn turned to follow Tom's gaze and shouted at him.

'Now didn't I tell you I'd sort this matter out, Mattie boy?'

The giant made no response except to pat the man tenderly on the shoulder and walk towards Tom and the doctor.

'I am pleased to make your acquaintance,' said Dr Harker, sounding a lot less confident than usual to Tom's ears.

'Matthew's a mute, sir,' said the man from the inn. 'Can't read nor write neither. So it'd be all the easier to pin some crime on him that he never done, what with him not able to gainsay it.'

Dr Harker nodded. 'Matthew,' he said. 'Do you know who killed poor Margaret?'

Matthew hesitated and then shook his head.

'Do you know who killed Bamberini the painter?'

Again the giant man shook his head.

'Do you swear you had nothing to do with either?'

Matthew nodded.

'Very well,' said the doctor. 'But there is just one other thing. Why did you attack Susannah Gibbs?'

Matthew shook his head and frowned and Tom wished the doctor had not asked the question. The giant's fingers wrapped themselves into enormous fists and he struggled to give voice to an answer that merely erupted as a rattling roar. To Tom's horror, the doctor persisted.

'Come now,' he said. 'Young Tom here saw you struggling with her. Mrs Gibbs had a cut on her forehead. You can hardly deny it.'

The giant suddenly marched towards Tom and grabbed him. Tom cried out, but as quickly as Matthew grabbed him, the giant pushed him away and fell to the floor flapping his hands about and pretending to sob.

There was something so bizarre and comical about this display that even the men who knew him were staring at Matthew in disbelief. He was clearly pretending to be Susannah Gibbs, but *why* was a puzzle to everybody.

Seeing that he had not made anyone understand, Matthew slapped the earth and stood up again. Again he strode over to Tom, again he pushed himself away, falling to the ground with the accompanying sobbing. Then he got up, pointed to his finger and slapped the back of his hand into his face.

'Matthew ain't simple, if that's what you're thinking,' said the man from the inn. 'He always means something. It's just it ain't always obvious.'

Matthew had risen to his feet and looked from face to face. When he saw that still no one understood he flung himself into a rage, kicking at the barn door and sending dust down from a beam over Tom's head.

'Matthew,' pleaded the man from the inn.

'Don't take on so. Try again, lad. We'll try harder.'
But Matthew was now standing off, his back to
them. Sullen and sulking.

'Matthew!' repeated the man. 'Don't be like
that, Matthew. We're here to help.'

'But do none of you know who might have
done these things?' interrupted Dr Harker. 'Even
with a drunken sheriff, it will not be long before
Matthew is arrested, even if only for the attack
on Mrs Gibbs.' Matthew groaned in the
background.

'I don't,' said the man from the inn. 'But Gibbs
has brought this on himself by meddling. He's a
good man, but he had no right disturbing that
grave and no good shall come of it. Some things
need leaving be.'

Dr Harker pointed at the masked men.

'Why the masks and the secrecy in bringing us
here?'

'We have professional reasons, sir,' said the
man with a smile.

'Smugglers!' said Tom, immediately wishing
he had not spoken.

'You are sharp, lad,' said the man from the inn.

Now Tom knew why Foley had been so reluctant to talk. 'My colleagues are involved in the importation business. We deal with the very best society, sir. Mr Fitzherbert for instance; he is very partial to his wine, he is. And your good friend Mr Gibbs too. Not that he won't have anything to do with us personal like. He leaves that to Foley.'

'Gibbs uses smugglers?' said Dr Harker in amazement.

'He do indeed, sir.'

'And that is how you met Margaret?' he said, turning to the giant.

Matthew nodded.

Dr Harker put out his hand. 'I am very grateful that you saved young Tom here from the creeks and very, very sorry for your loss.'

Matthew swallowed hard and his eyes became brighter. After a moment's hesitation he took the doctor's hand, shook it once and nodded.

'Now then,' said the man from the inn. 'Having heard what you need, you must be on your way, gentlemen. You are a danger to us by your presence as you will appreciate.'

Tom and Dr Harker's hoods were replaced and

Tom enjoyed the experience no more for having met their captors. Those sinister masked men seemed easily capable of – or possibly even *fond* of – murder.

They were bundled aboard a cart once more and covered again for their next journey. Eventually, the cart stopped and they were unceremoniously hauled onto their feet.

'I would be grateful to you gentlemen if you would say the Lord's prayer for me now,' said the by-now familiar voice of the man from the inn.

'Oh, for goodness sake,' said Dr Harker. Once again they heard the sound of pistols being cocked.

'Humour me,' the man said. 'And if you was wondering how come Matthew come to be a mute, you'll discover the cause soon enough if you breathe a word of what you just seen and heard.'

'Our Father who art in heaven,' they began.

'Good,' he said. 'Keep it up.'

When Tom and the doctor reached the end there was a silence around them until they heard slow shuffling footsteps approaching them. The sound got nearer and nearer until it stopped beside them and they heard a wheezy breathing.

Tom could stand it no longer and pulled his hood off to find the doctor had already done the same. They were standing near St Felix's church on the back lane. Dr Harker was staring at a hunchbacked old crone carrying a bundle of twigs. She was peering at them as though they had fallen from the moon.

'Good day, madam,' said Dr Harker, adjusting his wig. 'Come along, Tom, there's no time to stand about.'

As Tom set off behind Dr Harker, he heard a croaking chuckle behind him.

'Well, Tom,' said Dr Harker. 'It seems we are no closer to knowing the truth behind Bamberini's murder, or the murder of Margaret Dereham for that matter. I do not accept that Bamberini killed Margaret, and if the smugglers did not kill Bamberini, then who did? Not that we can necessarily believe a word the smugglers say. They are hardly known for their honesty now, are they?'

'Doctor Harker,' said Tom suddenly. 'I think I have an idea about Bamberini's killer, sir.'

Dr Harker stopped.

'Well let's hear it, Tom.'

'Well, sir, Foley says he saw Bamberini often on the back lane that leads to Lord Ickneld's house and, well, we know Lord Ickneld is obsessed with Redwulf. Maybe Bamberini was stealing the objects to give to Lord Ickneld.'

Dr Harker put his hand to his chin and sighed. 'That's possible of course,' he said. 'But I still don't see how that helps us with who killed him.'

'Well,' said Tom, 'Lord Ickneld is a big and powerful man, sir.'

'True.'

'And he has that big skull-handled cane,' continued Tom. 'That would make a fearsome weapon if wielded with force.'

'True again,' said Dr Harker. 'But why would he kill Bamberini if Bamberini was helping him?'

'I don't know,' said Tom, shaking his head.

Dr Harker suddenly stopped in his tracks and stared off into the marshes.

'Come on, Tom. We must pay a visit to Lord Ickneld!'

'Must we?' said Tom, seeing in his mind's eye in quick succession, Fenrir the hound, the skull-handled cane and Bamberini's body.

'Certainly!' said Dr Harker, already walking off in the other direction. 'And there is no time like the present!'

17

HALLOWEEN

Ickneld Hall was just as Tom had imagined it to be. It was squat and dark, like a crouching animal, surrounded by a weed-choked moat.

The roofline bristled with fat smoke-blackened chimneys and one wing of the house seemed to be wrapped round a tower that was encrusted with niches and decoration like those on a church. The windows were small and divided into narrow slits of leaded glass, the doorway arched and carved with grotesque figures and leering faces.

There seemed to be a lot of activity in the grounds of Ickneld Hall when Tom and the doctor arrived. Workmen were building a strange stone structure near a clump of holly trees, and near the creek there was a bonfire being constructed. Tom had a sudden and horrible memory of Gibbs's tales of sacrifices.

Lord Ickneld's manservant showed them in and Lord Ickneld greeted them like old friends.

'What an enormous pleasure,' he said, shaking them by the hand. 'We do not get many visitors.'

Tom was not at all surprised to hear it. The hall was as gloomy in appearance as its owner, hung all about with ancient weapons and shields and dark portraits of Lord Ickneld's ancestors. Fenrir padded about but seemed totally un-interested in Tom or the doctor, eventually settling himself down in front of the enormous fireplace.

'It seems very busy outside,' said Dr Harker.

'Yes,' said Lord Ickneld. 'I am having an ice-house built. Won't you sit down and Reynolds will get us all a drink.'

'And the bonfire?' said Dr Harker.

'Ah, yes,' said Lord Ickneld. 'Well it is All Hallow's Eve – Halloween. You town dwellers have lost touch with the seasons, my friends, but despite the suffocating grip of monks and priests, here time passes with some of its old marking.' Reynolds brought in a tray with a decanter of red wine and three glasses. Lord Ickneld poured them each a drink and then settled back in his chair.

'Halloween is a very ancient festival of course,' he continued. 'To the Celts it was the eve of winter; Samhain, the beginning of a New Year.' He took a sip of wine and his glass sparkled in the flamelight. 'It was a special time; a time when the laws of nature could be suspended and the spirits of the dead might be set loose to return to move among the living they once knew.' Tom shifted uneasily in his chair. 'The Christian missionaries denounced it as devil-worship of course, and did their usual trick of attempting to smother it by adopting it as their own, but on a night like Halloween it is easy to feel those pagan fears of the winter darkness.'

'You say Christian with such a tone of contempt to your voice, sir,' said Dr Harker.

'I apologise if I have offended you.'

'Not at all. I am merely interested.'

'I am English, sir,' said Lord Ickneld. 'I do not say that with contempt for those, like Signor Bamberini, who come from other lands. I have travelled widely. But I am of this land, and I have the old religion to sustain me. I have no need of such Levantine folk-tales.'

Tom looked to Dr Harker in bafflement.

'He means the Bible, Tom,' said Dr Harker. Tom looked shocked and Lord Ickneld smiled.

'You have no doubt heard that I worship the devil and am a wizard and so forth,' said Lord Ickneld. 'I can assure you I do not, though I must admit that when I was younger it amused me to shock my neighbours and I may have encouraged these tales.'

'We heard about sacrifices,' said Dr Harker.

'No,' said Lord Ickneld. 'No sacrifices, I am afraid. But I confess I am proud to call myself a pagan.'

'And how did the pagans you ally yourself with mark this festival?' Dr Harker asked.

'Well,' said Lord Ickneld, 'they lit huge bonfires for one thing. You saw mine in preparation by the creek. It is a tradition that has been largely stolen by Guy Fawkes Night, but we keep the old calendar alive. Firelight must be the oldest, the most ancient, of guards against the fears of the darkened corner. It is a comfort still, is it not?'

Tom looked into the fire and nodded as the wind boomed about the house.

'And it is not just ghosts that are supposed to take to the land of the living on Halloween, gentlemen,' Lord Ickneld continued. 'It is also a night in which the creatures of the dark world of our nightmares are free to roam. It is a night when charms can be invoked and futures divined. It is a night when supernatural happenings of all kinds are possible.' Tom swallowed hard and Lord Ickneld smiled at him.

'What do you know about Redwulf's grave?' said Dr Harker.

'Well, Doctor,' Lord Ickneld answered. 'As you probably already know from Gibbs, Redwulf was a warrior chieftain, one of the sea-kings of East Anglia eleven hundred years ago.

'When the Romans left, Christianity left with them, and a wave of immigrants from the Continent flooded in and restored what I consider to be the true religion of this country; a veneration of the natural forces and features of the land: of water, of trees, of the weather, of stones, and a worship of our ancestors.

'But Christianity came back. Missionaries came to this island; Augustine came from Rome and converted the men of Kent. Then Felix came to East Anglia. Redwulf refused to accept this foreign religion and was poisoned by one of the men of his own hall. He died a pagan, and became the focus of a warrior cult.

'Centuries later, a story appears that a knight returning from the Crusades had seen a vision of

St Felix who told him Redwulf had in fact converted to Christianity before he died, that he had been baptised in secret, which of course is nonsense, as there is not one single Christian artefact in the hoard so I am told. But this knight started a chivalric order to guard the grave. This is the origin of the Sentinel.'

'And do you believe in this Sentinel, Lord Ickneld?'

'I do not believe; I *know*,' he said, taking another sip of wine. Dr Harker was about to speak when Lord Ickneld held up his hand to stop him. 'I should not tell you this, Doctor, but I am going to anyway,' he continued. 'The Order of the Sentinel still exists to this day. I know because my father was a member of the Order.' Tom stared at Dr Harker. 'A Sentinel is chosen from its number every seven years, sworn to defend Redwulf's grave.'

'Is the Sentinel responsible for these killings?'

'He is not.'

'How do you know?'

'He is not the killer. I swear it,' said Ickneld putting his hand to his heart.

'Can you tell us who the Sentinel is?' said Tom.

'You have already met him,' said Ickneld with a raise of an eyebrow. 'You have already spoken to him. You have already looked him in the eye.'

18

THE SENTINEL

'I have already met him?' said Tom, shuddering slightly at the thought of the giant figure in the marsh.

'Yes,' said Ickneld with a smile. 'Sheriff Gerald Fitzherbert.' Tom and the doctor exchanged puzzled glances. Lord Ickneld laughed. 'Hard to believe, I realize. But I promise you it is true. Gerald is the Sentinel.'

'And you are sure he has nothing to do with the deaths?'

'Come now, gentlemen,' Ickneld said. 'You have met our sheriff. Gerald is a fine fellow in many ways, of course, but do you see him standing in a marsh fending off grave-robbers? I think not. No, no, the role of the Sentinel has become a mere honorary title,' he said a little sadly. 'It is an honour the recipient bears with great pride, but I fear you may have to look elsewhere for Redwulf's avenger.

'The Order long ago ceased to be the organization it once was. It began as a chivalric brotherhood, but I am sorry to say that it has descended into a quaint and harmless charitable body. They have an annual dinner where oaths are sworn and a great deal is drunk, but sadly the society members show little sign of punishing the desecrators of Redwulf's grave. In reality the task of protecting the barrow has fallen to my family on whose land the grave has always stood.

Until my father was forced to sell, of course.'

'Tom here thinks you may have killed Bamberini,' said Dr Harker.

Tom looked horrified but Lord Ickneld smiled.

'Does he now?' he said. 'I hope this is not because of Fenrir's attack on you. I have apologised for that.' Fenrir raised his head a little at the mention of his name but lay his muzzle back down between his paws with a sigh.

'No, sir,' said Tom. 'I just thought that . . . well, that is to say . . .'

'It is quite all right, Tom,' said Lord Ickneld. 'I am a pagan and therefore I must have no morals. I understand. Added to which I am a big man with a large cane and I know my way around the creeks. I dare say it could have been me. But it wasn't me. In any case I liked Bamberini. He was a frequent visitor here.

'I had seen one of his drawings and was impressed. A man of that talent does not happen by every day and I asked him if he might come and speak to me concerning the possibility of a portrait.'

'A portrait?' said Dr Harker. 'Of yourself?'

'No, no,' said Lord Ickneld with a smile. 'Of someone very dear to me. Bamberini slipped away whilst doing a sketch of the outside of Gibbs's house.'

'But why the secrecy?'

'Bamberini knew that Gibbs would not want to hear of him working for me,' said Ickneld. 'Besides, he was kind enough to bring me the drawings of the treasure hoard so that I could see the riches that Redwulf had taken with him. Gibbs would have dismissed him had he found out.'

'It was an odd friendship, was it not?' said Dr Harker. 'A Catholic and a pagan?'

'You must know little of the Catholics of Bamberini's land, Doctor,' said Lord Ickneld. 'Bamberini had a deep appreciation of the invisible world. He had a real understanding, too, of evil. He told me himself that he thought the maid had been murdered. He saw a wound on the back of her head and he saw a spade lying on the ground near the garden wall; a spade that had been leaning against that wall in the drawing he had begun before his visit to me that morning. He could not have killed the maid as I have heard suggested. He was here with me.'

'And when he was seen coming back he did not want to say where he had been,' said Dr Harker.

'Precisely,' said Ickneld. 'He was a little the worse for drink when he left here and stumbled in the mud by the moat. I fear that others may have put a more sinister meaning to his dirty stockings.'

Dr Harker nodded. 'So do you have any idea who may have killed Bamberini?' he urged.

'I will tell you that I cannot believe Matthew was responsible,' said Lord Ickneld. 'And I will say so at his trial if need be.' He smiled. 'You know the smugglers hint that they are responsible for his being mute, but he was born that way.'

'You know him?' said Tom.

'He has been to this house on many occasions. On errands of one sort or another.'

'For the smugglers,' said Dr Harker.

'For the smugglers, yes. I have a weakness for fine wine, I am afraid. But I do not have Gibbs's income.'

'Do you think the smugglers could have killed Bamberini?' Tom asked.

'They *could* have, yes,' said Lord Ickneld. 'They are ruthless enough. But even smugglers rarely kill without reason. Why would they have killed him?'

'Then do you have any theory at all?' said Dr Harker.

Lord Ickneld smiled and raised an eyebrow. 'You will think me fanciful I know, but before the Sentinel became a folkloric ritual, maybe it was something more real . . .'

'Come now, sir,' said Dr Harker dismissively.

'You need to live here, Doctor,' said Ickneld, the smile now gone from his face. 'You need to live with the marshes to know what I mean. You are not in London now, Doctor. You are barely in England.'

'What do mean by more "real"?' asked Tom.

'Well,' Ickneld began, 'before the Normans made a fey romance of the Redwulf legend, there was a different version of the tale. The story was that there was a fearsome creature living in the creeks who would emerge from the mud to challenge anyone unwise enough to cross them to a wrestling match. The creature was huge and powerful and always won, hurling his vanquished opponents into the mud to drown.

'Redwulf was told of this creature and strode fearlessly out to do battle with it. When the creature appeared, Redwulf threw down his helmet, sword and spear and vowed to fight the creature hand to hand. The monster grabbed him and locked him in its hellish embrace, but could not get the better of Redwulf. They wrestled on for seven days and seven nights, until the creature eventually let Redwulf go and said that never before had he ever met his match and that he would swear allegiance to this king. For his part Redwulf made the ogre promise to leave his people in peace and that if he did he could live there unharmed.

'When Redwulf was poisoned and buried in his grave with his treasure hoard, the creature rose from the mud of the creeks and climbed atop the barrow and wailed for days and nights on end. Then it called to Redwulf's kinfolk and told them his promise to leave them in peace died with

Redwulf. He would once again patrol the creeks and anyone who attempted to steal from or in any way desecrate the hero's grave would feel his wrath. This was his curse upon them and their children for evermore.'

'It is a fine tale,' said Dr Harker. 'But a fairy-tale all the same.' Lord Ickneld made no reply. 'You seriously believe the grave is cursed?'

'I do,' said Lord Ickneld.

'And yet you are still alive and well, sir.'

'Meaning?'

'Come now. It was you who took the bones from the barrow, was it not?' said Dr Harker. Lord Ickneld smiled. 'Your "ice house" is in fact a burial chamber, is it not?'

'Yes,' said Lord Ickneld after a moment's hesitation. 'Yes, it is. You really are a remarkable man, Doctor.'

'But why?'

'I will not stand idly by and see the grave of that great man desecrated,' said Lord Ickneld. 'Where is the respect? When does a man's grave become a toy for other men to amuse themselves with, Dr Harker? How would you feel if one day your bones were dug up and gawped at like some freak show at the fair?'

'But could you not have explained your feelings to Gibbs?' said Dr Harker.

'Gibbs?' said Lord Ickneld. 'I have tried. I even went to his house once to try and resolve our differences but that . . . that wife of his intercepted me at the door and made it very plain she thinks me unworthy of her husband's attention . . . In any case,' he added, 'why should I have to explain myself to Gibbs?'

'But then why are you explaining yourself to us?'

'Because you asked, and he did not. Because I like you, Dr Harker.' He smiled.

'Well, thank you for your time, Lord Ickneld,' Dr Harker said. 'Tom and I must be leaving.'

'Yes, of course,' said Ickneld. 'I hope I have been of some assistance.'

'You have been most informative,' said Dr Harker. Fenrir the wolfhound rose with a low growl and accompanied Ickneld as he showed Dr Harker and Tom to the door.

'Good day, gentlemen,' said Lord Ickneld.

Tom and Dr Harker walked back to Low House. They talked about all they had learned that day, but agreed that they must keep their peace once inside the house. Besides, the facts seemed to contradict themselves. One moment everyone seemed a suspect for the murders, the next no one did.

They said nothing of their adventure with the smugglers or their visit to Lord Ickneld. They had no wish to upset their hosts and Tom was happy to retire early to his bed. A grim atmosphere had descended on Low House and the creeks and it seemed hard to imagine how it might ever be lifted.

He had been asleep for barely five minutes when he suddenly felt compelled to get out of bed and go to the window. He pulled back the curtains and looked out over the creeks. A full moon appeared from behind a cloud and shone over the marshes, glinting on the water in the creeks and on the sea beyond the dunes.

As Tom watched, he caught sight of movement in the track leading down to the beach. Someone was walking towards the house with the slow, shuffling, child-like gait of a sleepwalker. There was something about the figure that chilled Tom's blood, but he could not tear himself away from the window.

But worse was to come. He heard a strange noise coming from the creek beyond the garden wall. The mud started to bubble up as if it were boiling, and then slowly and horribly, a head began to rise, the face deathly pale, its eyes open despite the mud dripping down.

Up and up the figure rose. Tom realized that this was Margaret Dereham. Despite the mud dripping down her face he recognized her from the drawing. She climbed completely out of the creek and stood on the back lane where she was joined by the other figure, who Tom saw clearly now was Bamberini, his head still bearing the wound, his face still caked with sand. A huge crow sat on his shoulder, croaking like a frog. Sand now fell horribly from Bamberini's mouth as he spoke.

'You know who did this!' he called
'I don't know!' whispered Tom.
'You know!' shouted Margaret Dereham. 'You know!'

'I don't!' shouted Tom. 'I swear!'

The figures ignored his shouts and instead began to walk towards the garden. Bamberini politely opened the gate for Margaret Dereham and Tom realized with mounting horror that they were heading towards the house. He ran to his door and opened it a crack. He heard the unmistakable sound of the latch being lifted on the garden door, and Margaret's squelching footsteps on the hall floor.

Tom shut the door and locked it. Tom backed away from the door, staring at the handle as he heard the ghoulish footsteps on the stairs getting closer and closer. The door handle moved. Only a little at first and then more impatiently. Then they began to bang on the door. Tom put his hands over his ears.

'I don't know!' he shouted. 'I swear I don't know!'

'Tom!' they shouted. 'Tom!'

'I don't know!' shouted Tom. 'Leave me alone!'

'Tom! It's me: Dr Harker! Are you all right!'

The door banged again and Tom woke up covered in sweat.

'Dr Harker!' shouted Tom, leaping out of bed, running to the door and unlocking it frantically.

'What is it, Tom?' said Dr Harker. 'Look at you. You are feverish. Come and sit down before you fall over.' Tom sat on the bed and tried to blink himself awake. 'What don't you know?' said Dr Harker.

'Sorry?' said Tom.

'You were shouting out that you did not know,' he said. 'Did not know what?'

'Oh,' said Tom. 'It was nothing, Doctor. Just a nightmare.'

'You are sure?' said the doctor.

'Quite sure,' said Tom.

19

ALL HALLOWS

Sheriff Fitzherbert visited Low House. Though more sober than before, he gave no better impression of himself. He had come to inform Mr and Mrs Gibbs that he had apprehended Matthew for the attack on Susannah and had taken him to the gaol in Lynn where he would be questioned about the murders of both Bamberini and Margaret Dereham. It had not been a difficult task to track down a man of Matthew's description, though few locally believed him capable of murder.

Dr Harker explained that Matthew was a mute and could not write but the sheriff waved these matters aside and said that Dr Harker should not worry himself about such an evident rogue and that justice would be served and Matthew would be hanged with all the due procedure.

When the sheriff had gone, Dr Harker continued his defence of Matthew but Susannah Gibbs rounded on him.

'Really, Dr Harker,' she said. 'That man attacked me and for all we know is guilty of far worse crimes. I would ask you not to side with him in my presence.'

'Nor mine,' said Gibbs. 'You are a fine man, Josiah, and you have a big heart, but I agree with Susannah. The man is clearly a brute.'

'I am not so sure,' said Dr Harker. 'There is something more to this business.'

'Come now, Josiah,' said Gibbs. 'The man could have killed Susannah had Tom not intervened. Who can tell why this creature behaved as he did? You are applying reason where none may exist. I say again, the man is a brute, Josiah.'

'Because he cannot speak?' said Dr Harker. 'Or because of his size? Neither factor is within the man's control, after all.'

'I am sorry, Josiah,' said Gibbs. 'I do not wish to be rude, but I cannot feel your sympathy for a man like that.'

'A man like that?' said Dr Harker. 'If you mean he was a smuggler, you did not seem to object when he was bringing contraband to this very house.' Gibbs opened his mouth to speak but no sound emerged. Dr Harker saw that he had gone too far. 'I am sorry, Abraham. That was ungenerous of me. I understand that this man stands accused of attacking your wife and it is a lot to expect for you to feel anything but harshness towards him. But I cannot help feeling that this man is nowhere near as bad as the company he keeps. Let us hope that your foundation may save others from a similar fate. After all, an education might have prevented Matthew becoming associated with these criminals.'

'If you are referring to the school, Josiah,' said Gibbs coldly, 'that project is at an end. I see now how things truly are. The kindness we have shown the people of this area has been thrown back in our faces time and time again. The whole population – from our own servants to Lord Ickneld – seems bent on driving us out. Well they shall have their wish, sir!'

'What can you mean, Abraham?'

'I mean, Josiah, that I am to sell Low House as soon as I am able and we shall be moving to London. I have business interests there, Josiah, and Susannah craves more society as you know. Well then. We shall not be missed, I dare say, but there you are. Good riddance to them all!'

Mr and Mrs Gibbs left Dr Harker and Tom alone and the doctor sighed and said to Tom that perhaps it was time that they went back to London themselves. He explained to Tom that though he felt sure that Matthew was no murderer he could offer no proof of his innocence and of his attack on Susannah there was no doubt at all, however strenuously he denied it. After all, Tom had seen it with his own eyes. Tom nodded in agreement, but though he had indeed seen the attack with his own eyes he was not as sure of it as he ought to have been.

It was not long before Gibbs returned. Tom was expecting a continuation of the previous disagreement, but Gibbs hurried eagerly over to shake their hands in turn and beg their pardon for his earlier ill temper. Susannah had persuaded him to make peace and he was forced to admit that he had been disagreeable. His mind was made up about leaving Norfolk, he told them, but that did not mean that they must depart on bad terms. Dr Harker agreed.

'Besides,' said Gibbs, 'tonight is the feast of All Saints, or All Hallows as we persist in calling it here. Though I'm sure you Londoners no longer take such notice of these things, here we like to mark our feast days. You must come to church tonight. I promise you it will be something you will be pleased not to have missed.'

Neither Tom nor Dr Harker were very keen to attend, but they did not feel able to refuse.

* * *

The scene that greeted them in the village street that evening was startling. As Tom, Dr Harker and Mrs and Mrs Gibbs reached the end of the drive a torchlit procession was walking past towards the church. The flames lit up the windows of the cottages, making the whole village shine.

The little church of St Felix shone like a jewel. The stained glass windows glowed like the intricate gemstone decorations on Redwulf's grave goods and inside there seemed to be a thousand candles burning defiantly against the cold dark void of the night. Lord Ickneld's pagan England seemed closer now to Tom, despite them entering a church. As if to confirm this, Lord Ickneld was there himself and walked over to greet them.

'Dr Harker,' he said warmly. 'How very nice to see you again. And you, Tom. Gibbs.'

'How dare you, sir,' hissed Gibbs. 'My wife has told me of your outrageous behaviour towards her.'

'I have no idea what you mean, I am afraid,' said Lord Ickneld.

'The day our servant died in the creeks,' said Gibbs. 'You had the ill manners to confront my wife in the lane.' Lord Ickneld opened his mouth to speak, but Gibbs waved him away. 'Please do not deny it, sir, or seek to excuse it. I will not bandy words with you.'

Susannah Gibbs sniffed and tugged at her husband's arm. 'Come, dear, let us sit down.'

With that Mr and Mrs Gibbs departed, leaving Lord Ickneld staring after them with one eyebrow raised.

'I had not thought to find you in a church, sir,' said Dr Harker.

Lord Ickneld frowned, still looking towards Susannah Gibbs. 'I am afraid I have a weakness for these old church rituals, Doctor,' he replied. 'The early Christians were sensible enough to see that religion is really about these simple things: light against dark, good against evil. I see no conflict in being here. Today and tomorrow, we remember the dead, in just the same way as our ancestors remembered *their* dead. It binds us to the past, does it not, Dr Harker? And maybe it makes us feel more alive, and treasure the life we have?' Dr Harker nodded. Tom became aware of a woman standing nearby, and Lord Ickneld beckoned her closer.

'Dr Harker. Mr Marlowe. May I introduce Miss Rachel Middleton?' he said. The woman stepped towards them and Tom and Dr Harker recognized her instantly from Bamberini's drawing. Tom realized that it must have been Miss Middleton whom Bamberini was to paint.

'I am delighted to meet you,' said Dr Harker.

'How do you do?' said Tom.

'I am very well thank you, Mr Marlowe,' said Miss Middleton.

'Miss Middleton and I have known each other since we were children, but she has only recently returned to the area. I was determined not to let her leave my side again and to my eternal surprise and wonderment she has very foolishly agreed to be my wife, gentlemen,' said Lord Ickneld. 'I have done my utmost to put her off, but there we have it.'

'Congratulations,' said Dr Harker. 'I hope you will be very happy together.'

'I rather think we shall,' said Lord Ickneld with a wide smile.

'Arthur speaks very highly of you, Dr Harker,' said Miss Middleton. 'And Arthur does not often speak highly of anyone.'

'Then I am honoured,' said Dr Harker.

'If you will excuse us, gentlemen,' said Lord Ickneld. 'We really ought to take our places.'

The service was solemn. The minister told them that this day and the following day – All Souls – were days in which they were to remember the dead; the illustrious dead like St Felix to whom the church was dedicated, but also the more recently departed. He made special mention of the recent tragic deaths at Low House and the congregation bowed their heads in a prayer of remembrance.

As they left to walk back to the house, the church bells of St Felix rang out and the wind carried the sound across the marshes and the creeks. Tom could hear others join them from other churches across the countryside as if the sound were echoing around the world and they were still ringing at midnight when Tom finally fell asleep.

20

ALL SOULS

Tom awoke the following morning in a reflective mood. The torchlit procession and the service in the little church was still fresh in his mind as was its concentration on the dead. It was the 2nd of November: All Souls.

210

Tom thought of his mother, and of his friend
Will Piggott, and tried hard to bring their faces
into focus in his mind. Sometimes it was hard to
remember them, but today he found that he could
see them both clearly as if they were closer to him
than they usually were. Today their memory
brought him comfort rather than sadness.

He had been trying to keep at bay the images
of Bamberini and Margaret Dereham from his
nightmare on Halloween, but now they crept
back in, unbidden. Again he heard their plaintive
cries of 'You know who did this!' and again Tom
whispered to himself that he did not.

Breakfast was very subdued. Tom knew they
must leave soon and so he decided to take a walk
down to the sea for what might be the last time.
Cloud shadows raced across the marshes and
where the sun shone on the dunes they were
bone-white.

He strolled along the beach, picking up shells
and throwing stones into the breakers, then
climbed to the top of a dune and sat amid the
shivering grass watching sea birds skim the waves.
There was neither a ship on the sea nor

another soul on the shore, and Tom felt alone in a way he had never felt in his life before. He lay back with his hands behind his head and looked up at the clouds rushing by and imagined it was he and not they who was moving; as if he were lying on the deck of a swift sailing ship with nothing about him but the endless sea.

When he finally walked back, Tom entered the courtyard wall by a side door, and was surprised to hear a cry. There was a stable boy lying on the ground, desperately backing away on his heels and backside, while Mrs Gibbs's horse Raven reared up in front of him.

The horse lifted up his front legs, flicking out his hooves and tossing his mane wildly. He snorted and whinnied and dropped his hooves to the cobbles with a noise like a pistol shot. Each time, the hooves got closer to the boy's legs.

Tom ran forward waving his arms and Raven backed off for an instant, startled by his sudden appearance. Tom darted forward and grabbed the stable boy, helping him to his feet. Putting his arm around his shoulders, he began to walk him away.

No sooner had they begun to do so, however,

than Tom heard the sound of hooves behind them and he just managed to drag the boy sideways and avoid being trampled himself. Raven cantered round the courtyard and prepared to charge again.

'Raven!' shouted Susannah Gibbs, stepping into the courtyard. 'Raven!' The horse turned to the sound of the voice and trotted away, as docile as a carthorse. Susannah led him a few yards away, chiding him gently, and tied him to a post. She was carrying a canvas bag and came over to Tom, who was still rooted to the spot. She wagged her finger at the stable lad.

'How many times have I told you to leave Raven to me, you silly boy! You were lucky you weren't hurt.'

'He was lucky he wasn't killed,' said Tom.

'Go and see Mr Foley and get yourself cleaned up,' Susannah Gibbs said to the stable boy before turning once more to Tom. 'I am so sorry,' she said. 'Raven is rather wild as you know. He won't even let Abraham near me.' She laughed and walked across to Raven, untied him, stroked his face and patted him.

The muscles in Raven's flanks twitched and his tendons quivered like bowstrings. His powerful neck flexed and arced, sending flickers of light shooting down its glossy surface, as smooth as polished jet.

Then suddenly, like scenes illuminated by lightning flashes, images from the past days at Low House burst unbidden into Tom's mind. He saw Raven's hooves flailing out and stomping down at the cobbles. He saw Bamberini's body, his face covered with blood and sand. He heard Dr Harker saying it was hard to believe it was the work of a human being. He saw the crow on Bamberini's shoulder in his nightmare, but now he knew it was no crow; it was a *raven*! Tom stared at Susannah Gibbs as she walked towards him.

'Why, Tom,' she said, 'whatever is the matter. You look as though you've seen a ghost.'

'It was *you*!' he said. '*You* killed Bamberini!'

'Yes,' she said. The smile remained. 'He was a frightful bore. You will not make me feel guilty for his death, Tom. No one liked him. *You* did not like him.'

'I would not have wished him dead!'

Susannah merely closed her eyes.

'But why?' said Tom.

'He leaped out at me in the dunes, the ridiculous man,' said Susannah. 'He said he knew that I had not met Lord Ickneld the morning of Margaret's death because he was with him. He said that I could not have been walking on the back lane because he was on the lane himself. I told him that it was simply his word against mine and he became irate and began babbling in that ugly language of his. Raven is very protective.' She looked fondly towards the stables.

Tom was puzzled by the significance of who was on the back lane and why, and then he realized what Bamberini had realized: that she was lying about this for a reason.

'You . . . You . . . You killed Margaret as well!'

'Stop it, Tom,' said Mrs Gibbs. 'You look at me as if I were a savage! I only wished to turn Abraham against these wretched people and this awful place. Margaret discovered me scratching the words on the wall. She said she knew I had never been attacked in the street and she cursed me for being a liar. She threatened to tell

Abraham. There was a spade. I picked it up and the next thing I knew she was sinking into the mud. I never intended to kill her. I had no choice.'

'Of course you did!' shouted Tom. 'Of course you did!'

'She was a servant!' cried Susannah Gibbs. 'And not a very good one. I gave her gifts and treated her well and she showed me no loyalty at all. I can't say I am proud of killing her, but I have not lost one wink of sleep over it.'

Tom stared at her as if he were only just that moment seeing her clearly.

'You have no right to look at me in that impertinent manner!'

'You are insane!' shouted Tom.

'Oh pish, Tom! You do talk nonsense.'

'You are insane!' Tom repeated.

Susannah Gibbs laughed loudly. 'And there I was thinking you were sweet on me, Tom Marlowe,' she said. 'How fickle you are.' She suddenly swung the bag at him. Tom was not expecting the blow or for the bag to be so heavy. It struck him in the nose and Susannah Gibbs and the creeks beyond disappeared in a shower of stars as he fell backwards.

Susannah mounted her horse. Tom was dimly aware of the horse's hooves and, remembering Bamberini, crawled away in panic for fear of being trampled. His face was wet. He tasted blood. He tried desperately to focus. A hoof landed inches from his head and he managed to scramble to the garden gate and throw himself through. A hoof clanged against the wrought iron as he did so.

'Tom!' shouted Dr Harker, running down the path to his side.

'I'm all right, sir,' said Tom, blinking and trying to gather the crowd of Dr Harkers into one sharp image.

Susannah screamed with rage and turned Raven away. Then Tom saw Gibbs standing over him, staring wildly.

'What is going on?' he said. 'Susannah! Susannah!'

'Can you stand, Tom?' asked Dr Harker.

'Yes, sir. I think so.'

Gibbs was already out of the garden and Tom

could see Susannah riding off towards the beach. Her way was blocked by a cart and a group of cockle diggers back from the beach. She switched direction and thundered by the house along the back lane heading towards the church. They ran in pursuit to find Susannah's way had been blocked once more.

Lord Ickneld was standing in the lane with Fenrir. The hound was straining at his leash, snarling at the horse and rider. Susannah swung Raven round and saw them coming. She jerked at the reins and turned towards the marsh. With a kick, she forced the horse to jump the creek in front of her.

The tide was almost out and there was only a trickle of water in the creek. Raven cleared the mud easily, but this manoeuvre only found them on an island surrounded by yet more mud.

'What the devil is going on?' shouted Gibbs. 'What are you doing there, Susannah? And you!' he shouted, pointing at Lord Ickneld. 'How dare you come here and frighten my wife.'

'Oh do be quiet, Abraham!' shouted Susannah Gibbs. 'You are making yourself ridiculous.'

Gibbs looked about him from face to face.

'Will someone tell me what's going on!'

'It's me, my sweet,' said Susannah. 'I am your murderer. I am your thief.'

'What?' cried Gibbs. 'What nonsense is this?'

'I murdered Margaret!' his wife shouted. 'I killed Bamberini! I scratched the words on the garden wall! I stole the grave goods and I put them on their bodies to make it look as though they were killed because of the barrow! It was all me! All your sweet silly Susannah.' She laughed. 'Look at your face, Abraham!'

'What are you saying?' Gibbs demanded. 'You? How could you have killed Bamberini? I saw his body. You could never have struck with such a force. Why are you talking such nonsense, Susannah?'

His wife patted her horse's neck. 'No, I could not strike such a blow, but Raven could and did,' she said. 'That awful man was going to tell you that I had killed Margaret.'

'What? I don't understand. In heaven's name, why did you kill Margaret?'

'I never meant to,' she said. 'But she saw me.

She was always out in the creeks for some god-forsaken reason and she saw me scratching the words into the stone and she told me that she knew I hadn't been attacked in the street either, the little sow!'

'You weren't attacked? I don't understand.'

'Oh, Abraham!' she laughed. 'Of course I wasn't. Tell him, Tom.' Tom said nothing. 'And I wasn't attacked by that giant oaf either. He stood there like an idiot groaning away and I heard someone coming so I grabbed him and pretended he was attacking me. He was trying to get away. It was really rather amusing. For good measure I gave myself a little scratch with the lovely diamond ring you bought me, my sweet. It was too perfect. And Tom was *so* brave.'

Tom realized now what Matthew had been trying to mime to them, and what his frantic pointing at his hand had meant. Gibbs again asked his wife to explain.

'Because I was bored!' she screamed. 'Bored with this godforsaken place, bored with my life and bored with *you*! It's all your fault! If you would only have agreed to move to London . . . or

even back to Bristol – anywhere but here! If anyone is to blame, it is you, Abraham Gibbs! I swear
you're more in love with your silly burial hoard
than you are with me!'

Susannah Gibbs pulled Redwulf's sword from
the bag hanging from the saddle and Tom's hand
instinctively went to his bloody nose. Now he
knew why it was so heavy.

'Here is your precious sword!' she shouted.

At that moment Raven whinnied and jittered,
as if he saw someone across the creek. His eyes
bulged and rolled, but more from terror than fury
it seemed to Tom. He followed the horse's gaze,
but there was nothing there.

Susannah Gibbs pleaded with the horse to be
still, gently at first but more and more
desperately as she lost control. Raven reared up,
kicking out with his forelegs, slithering in the wet
mud and lurching sideways, throwing Susannah
Gibbs into the creek along with the treasure
hoard, which tipped out of the bag and began
disappearing into the mud. Susannah cried out as
she began to sink. Tom was the first to rush forward, but the horse bounded between him and

Mrs Gibbs, head bowed and ready to butt him. Abraham and Dr Harker tried to intervene but Raven would not let them pass. He reared up again and lashed out wildly with his hooves. Through the horse's legs, Tom could see Susannah Gibbs, the sword above her head, neck deep in mud. The next moment there was only the sword. Then there was only mud.

The instant Susannah Gibbs disappeared from sight, the horse calmed himself, shaking his mane and snorting as if coming out of a trance. Then he became still, looking back towards the marsh. The next thing Tom knew, Abraham Gibbs was throwing himself headlong into the creek yelling 'Susannah!' at the top of his lungs. Within seconds he was sinking too.

Lord Ickneld rushed forward with Tom quickly at his side and together they pulled Gibbs from the mud. When they had him out, he immediately struggled free and tried to return to his search for Susannah. When Tom's attempts to stop him failed, Foley suddenly appeared, stepped forward and punched Gibbs on the jaw, knocking him unconscious.

'Er . . . thank you,' said Tom. Foley grunted.

Foley fetched a boat hook, but search as they might, they never did find Susannah Gibbs's body, or the sword. Gibbs came to in a minute or so and sat on the ground staring at the smooth surface of the mud while Raven pawed the earth beside him.

21

FAREWELLS

A few days later Tom and Dr Harker walked
out along the track to the beach, the ink-
black night pierced by thousands of stars. Little
was said by either of them. Tom's head was
buzzing with the memories of recent events.

Matthew had been released from prison now that the truth was known about his alleged attack on Susannah Gibbs. The authorities had wanted to hold him anyway on the grounds that he had known links with smugglers, but Lord Ickneld had used his influence to have him set free without any further delay.

But such good news seemed small comfort put beside the sadness of the past few days and Tom's mind inevitably turned to Susannah Gibbs and the cold seemed to sting his eyes more keenly and the stars to blur and twinkle.

Tom and the doctor stayed to attend the service for Susannah at St Felix's church. They walked with Gibbs to the churchyard and were all surprised to find Lord Ickneld waiting for them. After some hesitation he and Gibbs shook hands and the four of them went into the church together.

Gibbs had hoped to keep the truth of Susannah's death from her family, but the network of servant gossip had passed the tale all the way to Bristol by the time of the funeral and her family had declined his invitation to attend. Tom wondered at how cold the church now seemed after the splendid candlelight of All Hallows. It was as if the magic had left the building.

After the service, Gibbs insisted on inviting Lord Ickneld to come to Low House and he accepted. They all walked back along the lane together and sat in front of the fire. The conversation was sparse, with Gibbs and Lord Ickneld still far from comfortable in each other's company. After a while, Gibbs rose and asked if they might excuse him, explaining that he needed to be alone for a while.

'It is a sad business,' said Lord Ickneld when he had gone.

'Yes indeed,' said Dr Harker. 'It will be hard for Abraham when we return to London, I fear.'

'Yes,' agreed Lord Ickneld.

'I wonder if I might beg a favour of you, Lord Ickneld?' said Dr Harker.

'Of course. What is it, Dr Harker?'

'I wonder if you might look in on Abraham, from time to time?' said Dr Harker.

Lord Ickneld smiled his now familiar wry smile. 'I should be happy to, if I would be welcome.'

'I rather think that you may,' said Dr Harker. 'At any rate, you will try?'

'You have my word on it,' said Lord Ickneld.

'Excellent,' said Dr Harker.

'There are some things I still don't understand, sir,' said Tom. 'For instance, how did Mrs Gibbs steal the grave goods and the sword? The library door was locked and Mr Gibbs was sure the lock had not been tampered with.'

'Abraham was right. No one had touched that lock except Abraham himself. Apart from you that is, Tom.'

'Me?' said Tom, looking a little worried.

'Yes, Tom. It happened the day Susannah was supposedly attacked,' said Dr Harker. 'You were given the key to the library, do you remember? You left her in the room alone, do you remember?'

'Yes, sir,' said Tom. 'But only for five minutes and she was locked in. I think I would have noticed if she had the treasure hoard hidden about her person when we left.'

Dr Harker smiled. 'But that's just it,' he said. 'She did not need to take the artefacts away then. She simply hid them.'

'Hid them?' said Tom. 'Where?'

'Behind the books, I imagine,' said Dr Harker. 'Then, when she came to clear up the vase she had intentionally broken, she took the hoard out in a basket. You see Abraham had no need to lock the library now because as far as we were all concerned, the treasure was gone.'

'To think,' said Tom. 'If Mr Gibbs had taken a book from a shelf he might have discovered the trick.'

'Indeed he would, Tom,' said Dr Harker. 'Susannah needed to get rid of the treasure before it was found. I think when you met her on the day of her death she was intending to dump it in the creek. After all she had won and no longer needed it. Gibbs had agreed to move to London. Her possession of the grave goods only incriminated her.'

Tom nodded, then turned to Lord Ickneld. 'Did you suspect the truth about Mrs Gibbs, sir?' he asked.

'I never liked her, Tom, it is true,' Lord Ickneld replied. 'She was wary of me because her charm did not work on me as it so clearly did on others.'

Tom felt himself blush a little. 'But no, I did not think her capable of murder. Not until the All Hallows service at St Felix.'

'What happened on All Hallows?' asked Dr Harker.

'Gibbs chastised me for being rude to his wife on the day Margaret Dereham was killed, but I had not seen her at all that day. As you know, Bamberini was with me that morning. I surmised that if Bamberini had walked back to the house along the back lane, he too would know that Susannah Gibbs was lying, and like me would wonder why. He made the fatal mistake of confronting her about it.'

'Still,' said Dr Harker. 'You must own that you were wrong about the Sentinel and the curse.'

'Must I?' said Lord Ickneld.

'Come now, sir,' said Dr Harker. 'We know that Margaret and Bamberini were victims of Mrs Gibbs's murderous intrigues, and we all saw Susannah fall from her horse. She was not killed by the curse.'

'We shall have to agree to differ in this matter,' said Lord Ickneld. Tom remembered Raven's terrified expression and felt more sympathy with Lord Ickneld's point of view than with Dr Harker's. 'Who are we to say how the curse is carried out? Gibbs has certainly paid a heavy price for breaking into the barrow, has he not?'

Dr Harker nodded.

'Sadly, on that we can agree.'

'Incidentally, sir,' said Tom. 'What was it that you were reciting over Bamberini's grave on the day of his funeral?'

'Ah,' said Lord Ickneld. 'Nothing sinister, I assure you. That was the Florentine poet Dante Alighieri. Do you know his work?'

Tom shook his head and said that he did not.

'You should, you know. He is really rather wonderful. Bamberini was very fond of Dante:

'Love weeps; so, lovers, come and weep likewise,
And stay to learn the reason for his tears.

'Dante lived four hundred years ago,' continued Lord Ickneld. 'But four hundred years or a thousand, he knew about love and the loss of love. And after all, gentlemen, what else is there when all is said and done?'

Lord Ickneld eventually said farewell to Tom and Dr Harker and about half an hour later, Gibbs reappeared. He apologized for leaving them alone and hoped that Lord Ickneld had not thought him rude. They assured him that he had nothing to reproach himself about and the three of them moved into the garden to look out over the marshes.

'I have decided to stay,' said Gibbs, gazing into the distance. 'And I am going ahead with the school. I intend now to call it the Margaret Dereham Memorial School. It is at least something . . .'

'Good man,' said Dr Harker. 'Your father would be proud.'

'I hope so,' said Gibbs. 'And I have wronged Lord Ickneld. I hope that I can set that to rights also.' Dr Harker nodded. 'I intend to give back some of the land my father took from the Icknelds. The barrow will return to his care and that can only be right. Maybe Redwulf's ghost will rest in peace.'

'You know, you have a lot more in common with Lord Ickneld than you seem to realize,' said Dr Harker. 'You both have a passion for this country's past. You both have a love of this land. You could have a friend there, Abraham.'

'You seem to admire him, Josiah,' said Gibbs. 'I had thought a rational man like you could find no common ground with a man like that.'

'I hope I would never be so rational a man that I would be blind to magic if it appeared before me,' said Dr Harker. 'Nor so rational that I would not admit that my heart is as sensitive to the pull of love and fear as any ancient pagan.'

Gibbs smiled.

'We modern men are in danger of wearing our reason like a suit of armour, Abraham,' said Dr Harker. 'But armour can be dented. It can be pierced.' Gibbs nodded. 'Lord Ickneld is a good man at heart, pagan or no. I am certain of it.'

'Ah,' said Gibbs, looking over Tom's shoulder. 'And here is someone else I need to mend bridges with . . .'

Tom looked round and saw Matthew walking towards them from out of the marsh.

'One moment,' said Gibbs, setting off back to the house.

Matthew strode over to Tom and the doctor and shook both their hands, nodding. Despite his lack of speech, he made his gratitude very plain. Gibbs came trotting back down the garden steps with a small box. He gave it to Matthew who took it with a look of puzzlement and opened the box with surprising delicacy. Inside was a necklace.

'It belonged to Margaret,' said Gibbs. 'I am sure she would have wanted you to have it.'

Matthew had tears in his eyes as he held it in front of his face. He nodded his thanks and shook Gibbs's hand and then placed the necklace around his own neck, tucking it inside his shirt and holding it there over his heart. Matthew nodded again and walked away towards Foley who was standing nearby.

'Rather a fine necklace for a maid,' said Dr Harker.

'I bought it for Susannah,' said Gibbs. 'But she

never liked it and gave it to Margaret. At first I was annoyed, but when I saw how much pleasure it gave Margaret to wear it, I felt only a kind of sadness that Susannah could not have felt the same. I suppose I did not really know her, if truth be told, Josiah.'

'Maybe she did not want to be known, Abraham,' said Dr Harker, patting Gibbs on the back. Gibbs turned and walked towards Foley and Matthew who were embracing like lost brothers.

'Well, Tom,' said Dr Harker. 'Our relaxing sojourn away from the hectic bustle of the Metropolis did not go quite as planned.'

'No, sir,' said Tom with a grim smile. 'It did not.'

'Poor Margaret,' said Dr Harker. 'Poor Bamberini. And poor Susannah Gibbs for that matter.'

'I can't bring myself to care too much about Susannah Gibbs,' said Tom.

'And yet you were fond of her, Tom. Man to man; you were fond of her, were you not?'

Tom looked at his feet. 'Yes I was,' he

said after a pause. 'But it was a lie I was fond of.'

'Few things in life are all lie or all truth, Tom,' said Dr Harker.

'Maybe so,' said Tom. 'I just wish . . .'

'Yes, Tom?'

'I just wish that it hadn't been her,' he said. 'That's childish, isn't it?'

'Not childish at all,' said Dr Harker, patting him on the shoulder. 'Come, Tom, let's go inside. My bones are cold.'

Tom smiled and the doctor turned and headed through the garden gate towards the house. Just before he followed him, Tom looked over towards the marsh and was surprised to see that Matthew was already some way off, silhouetted against the dunes, looking back towards the house, his hair waving in the chill breeze. Tom waved, but to his surprise he made no response.

Then, as he turned to go through the gate, he saw Matthew still standing with Gibbs and Foley who were locked in conversation. Tom whirled round to look at the marshes but there was nothing there.

'Doctor!' shouted Tom as he stared out in disbelief.

'Did you call, Tom?' said Dr Harker, reappearing in the doorway. Tom stared out into the empty marshes.

'Tom?'

'No . . . Sorry, sir,' said Tom. 'I thought I . . . I was mistaken . . .'

Dr Harker peered at him, and followed his gaze out across the marshes. 'Very well,' he said. 'Then with your permission I shall warm my frozen backside by the fire. We shall have quite a tale to tell our friends when we get back to London, shall we not?'

'Yes,' said Tom staring into the marshes. 'We certainly will.'

If you enjoyed *Redwulf's Curse*, you'll love the other Tom Marlowe books. In Tom's first adventure with Dr Harker, the two friends investigate the mystery of the bodies that have been discovered around the city of London, each pierced by an arrow and left holding a strange card . . .

Turn over to read the first two chapters of *Death and the Arrow* . . .

1

MURDER IN THE TOWN

It was an April morning in 1715. Ludgate Hill was in full flow. Carriages and carts clattered over the slippery cobbles and a thousand busy feet pounded the pavements. It was barely noon but the street was as dark as dusk, as chimney after chimney puffed and spluttered like a sailor in a gin cellar.

A surgeon sniffed at the perfumed handle of his cane, trying to rid his nose of the mortuary stink, and cheered himself with the thought that there was a hanging tomorrow and he had been promised the corpse. An African, stolen by slavers from his native land, tried unsuccessfully to recall his people's word for sun. A red kite flew across the smoke-stained sky, trailing the bloody proceeds of a scavenging trip to Smithfield market. A soldier patted a sweep for luck. A wig-maker from Cheapside searched for his watch and finding his pocket empty shouted, '*Stop, thief!*' Gentlemen felt for their sword hilts, villains for their clasp knives. A constable cursed and ducked down an alleyway, but the pickpocket was long gone.

Hawkers of every kind called out, 'Oranges!' and 'Oysters!' and 'Won't you buy my . . .' this or that, until the air was filled with their deafening jabber and you could not tell who was selling milk and who was selling mousetraps.

And there, in the midst of all this, was Tom

Marlowe, fifteen years old, an apprentice at his father's printing shop under the sign of the Lamb and Lion in Fleet Street. Mr Marlowe printed all manner of things: posters and pamphlets, sermons and ballads – even the 'Last Dying Speeches' of the condemned.

Tom was taking a bundle of proofs of a scientific pamphlet to Dr Harker at his coffee house, The Quill, in St Paul's churchyard. The new cathedral towered above, its stonework still stark and soot-free, its great lead dome visible for miles around. Tom's father hated it. 'A dome?' he had said when it was finished. 'Are we Italians? No! A spire, Tom, a tower – that's England, boy.'

Tom, on the other hand, thought it the most amazing thing he had ever seen and never tired of looking at it.

Warm air swept over him as he opened the coffee-house door and a couple of the customers rustled their newspapers, irritated by the intrusion. Dr Harker was in his usual place over by the fire.

'Tom, lad,' he called and motioned with his cane for Tom to come and join him. 'A bowl of chocolate for my young friend! Sit yourself down, lad. How's your father, Tom?'

'He's well, thank you, Dr Harker.'

Dr Harker was Tom's favourite of all his father's customers and the doctor was, in his turn, very fond of the young apprentice. The doctor's own son was a navy man; he was away at sea most of the time and showed little interest in his father or his work when he was home. 'What is the point in knowing more than you *need* to know?' asked the son on his last visit. 'But I *need* to know *everything*!' answered the father. They were a puzzlement to each other.

But Tom could listen to the doctor all day long. He was so clever – 'stuffed full of learning', Mr Marlowe called him – and he had *done* so much. In his younger days he had sailed to the Americas and Africa and had dozens of cabinets chock-full of the curiosities he had found there. When he talked, he would wave his arms in the air, as if trying to catch the visions he was conjuring up for his young friend, and the curls of his periwig would shake, dusting his coat with powder.

It was magical for Tom. He had never done anything or been anywhere. His life, or so he felt, was as dull as the Fleet ditch and looking into Dr Harker's life was like looking into a sparkling jewel box.

'Another brandy,' said a voice to their right, 'to warm these old bones of mine.' It was the Reverend Purney, the chaplain of Newgate jail. He nodded over at Tom, took out his long clay pipe and flashed his yellow teeth; Purney was another of Mr Marlowe's clients.

'It would take a gallon of brandy to warm that hypocritical old buzzard,' whispered Dr Harker. 'Do you know what hypocritical means, Tom?'

'No, sir, I don't,' replied Tom.

'And long may it remain so,' said Dr Harker with a grin. 'Long may it remain so.'

At that moment a youth burst in with an armful of newspapers. 'Murder in the town!' he shouted – to no great effect, for murders were all too common in these violent times. '*Extraordinary* murder!' he called, perhaps a little disappointed at the response.

'How so?' called a wag by the window. 'Have

they caught the murderer then?' The coffee-house client-ele erupted into laughter.

'Beskewered by an arrow right through his heart, that's how so!' replied the youth. He had their attention now.

'An arrow?' said Dr Harker quietly to no one in particular. 'Now that *is* rather unusual.'

'It's the work of the Mohocks, I'll be bound!' said the Reverend Purney, and there was a grumbling of agreement. The newspapers had been full of horror stories about the gang of upper-class thugs.

'I think not,' said Dr Harker.

'Oh?' said Purney. 'And why not? They name themselves after savages and behave like savages. Murder with arrows would seem a logical step.'

'What difference does it make?' said a young man nearby. 'With lords for fathers and uncles in the government, they're never going to be chatting to you in the Condemned Hold, now are they, Reverend?'

Several people nodded and said, 'That's right,' but Dr Harker ignored this diversion.

'The Mohocks cannot be ruled out, I agree.

But we need more information. Do you have any other facts for us, lad?' he called to the youth.

'I do, sir! There's witnesses what say that this here skewered gent runs past them seconds before the deed, and on into a courtyard with no way out but locked doors – locked, mark you. They follows him and finds him nailed ... but not another soul in sight! Not a sparrow, not a tick.' A murmur ran round the room.

'But there's more,' said the youth, pointing his finger at no one in particular. 'It turns out that this here stiff was dead already.'

'Dead already?' said Dr Harker. 'What do you mean?'

'Well, sir,' replied the newspaper boy, smiling now that he had his audience in his grip, 'this here corpse – Leech was his name – he was a soldier-boy, fighting the French in the Americas, God save the King.'

'Yes, yes,' said Dr Harker impatiently. 'To the point, lad!'

'Well, it's like I was just saying. A military man, he was, and paid the price. Cut down by heathen savages. Murdered by Indians out in the

Americas while he was fighting the French some years ago!' Tom's eyes widened.

'What?' said Purney. 'Impossible!'

'Killed him dead, they did, and all the men with him.'

'Then there must be a mistake,' said the owner of the coffee house. 'The murdered man must be someone else.'

'No, sir. No mistake. His own mother lives not a spit away and verified him with her own teary eyes. His sergeant come down and did the same. There ain't no mistake.'

The customers began to mutter to themselves and mumble asides at their neighbours, but the newspaper boy held up his hand. 'And ask me how the Indians killed them. Go on, ask me.'

'Shot by arrows?' suggested Dr Harker.

'Arrows it was,' said the youth. The customers gasped and turned to the doctor in amazement.

'Come now,' he said with a shrug. 'It hardly took a genius to divine that if he had been killed by natives, they might use bows.' Even so, Tom noticed Dr Harker turned back to the newsboy with a contented smile. 'Is there more?' he asked.

'There is,' he was told. 'In his pocket they finds a card – a calling card, if you like. And you ain't never going to guess what was on it!'

There was a long pause – rather too long – and Dr Harker was forced to break the silence by saying, 'I rather fear that we won't. Could you do us the enormous favour of telling us?'

The coffee house filled with laughter again and the newspaper-seller blushed. 'In his pocket they finds a card,' he repeated, 'and on that card there's an embellishment – a figure of Death, no less, pointing one bony finger and looking like to chuck an arrow with the other hand. Now, gents, tell me if that ain't a story or what?'

Even the sour-faced Reverend Purney had to admit that it *was* quite a story – though one could not always believe what one heard or even what one read in the newspapers. He reminded the customers – again – that he had once heard a report of his own body being found floating in the Fleet. Everyone nodded and smiled, but several customers secretly hoped to see that report proved true.

2

Fog

By the time Tom left the coffee house, a thick sulphurous fog had taken hold of the city. It was the queasy colour of curdled milk and gripped his throat like a thief. He could see almost nothing in the murk and kept to the wall, dodging the other poor citizens as they coughed their way blindly towards him. He could hear the muffled clatter of horses' hooves and the *tick, tock* of walking sticks and boot heels; somewhere in the distance cattle were lowing as they made their way to market, and the smells of baking bread, fish, coffee and horse dung competed with the rotten-egg stink of the fog.

Tom had no fear of getting lost – he could make this journey blindfolded – but he kept up a brisk pace all the same, thinking all the while about arrows and Indians and murdered men. But most of all he thought about that hideous figure of Death, and shivered to his bones.

In this state of mind, Tom could be forgiven for letting out a shriek when a hand reached out from a doorway and almost pulled him off his feet. There was a peal of rough laughter and then a cough like nails shaken in a rusty pot. It was Will.

Whenever Tom went out on business these days, his father shouted, 'And mind who you're talking to, lad!' And though no one was mentioned by name, they both knew that it was Will who Tom's father had in mind.

Mr Marlowe thoroughly disapproved of Will and would fly into a rage at the mere mention of his name. He could not understand what a lad like Tom could possibly want with the company of such a rogue as Will. And rogue he certainly was.

'Why can't you just say hello like everyone else?' said Tom, smiling now.

'What's with the screaming, Tom? I thought for a minute I'd grabbed a Frenchman by mistake!' Will wheezed and spat on the ground.

'Very funny, Will, very funny. I wonder you don't get yourself a booth at Bartholomew Fair and make yourself some *honest* money, you being such a clown and all,' said Tom, giving Will a shove in the arm.

'Now, now – no need for that. But you won't rile me, Tom, for I've had a good day.'

'Give it back,' said Tom with a sigh.

'What?' pleaded Will. 'I ain't done nothing.'

'The watch, Will. Hand it over.'

'I don't believe it! There's no way you could've felt it. How come you knew, Tom? How? I'm a master, I am. I could take the ring from a bull's nose, with him none the wiser. I just can't see how you could've felt that — I just can't . . .'

Will muttered away to himself and kicked out at the wall. Tom had felt nothing — Will was every bit the master of his art he claimed to be, but he had taken to picking Tom's pocket every time they met and Tom now merely guessed and heartily enjoyed the effect it had on his friend.

Will handed back the pocket watch. A grin suddenly shone out from his grimy face. 'Come on.' And so the two of them walked on together through the fog, each, as usual, fascinated by the other's very different life; Tom recalling, yet again, the part his pocket watch had played in their first meeting . . .

Their friendship had begun one August a couple of years before, at Bartholomew Fair in Smithfield. Tom loved the fair. There was just so much to see: jugglers and fire-eaters, tightrope walkers and conjurors; there were gypsies too, like parrots come to rest among sparrows, with their gold earrings and rainbow clothes.

Tom had been standing at the edge of the fair listening to a strange character dressed in sackcloth preaching about the end of the world, when he heard a commotion behind. He had turned just in time to see a driverless horse and carriage rushing towards him.

He had not even had time to call out before he was knocked off his feet; he hit the pavement with a winding thud. But he had not been mown down by the horse or the carriage; he had been pushed out of their path and into a side alley.

Tom looked up at the dirty face of his saviour. 'Y-you saved my life,' he stammered.

'You know, I reckon you might be right at that,' said the lad with a grin. They got to their feet and dusted themselves down.

Tom held out his hand and smiled. 'Tom Marlowe,' he said.

'The name's William Piggot,' said Will with a grin, 'but most people call me—'

'A thieving little cockroach,' said a voice behind them.

They turned to see a tall man dressed in black looming over them, a billowing powdered wig under his tricorn hat, one hand on the hilt of his silver sword. Behind him were two other men, also dressed in black.

'Mr Hitchin, sir . . .' began Will, his face a little paler under the grime.

'That's Under-marshal Hitchin to you, scum,' said the tall man. 'Make sure we are not disturbed.' This was directed at his companions, who retreated to block the entrance to the alley.

Hitchin's sneer suddenly became a crocodile grin as he turned to Tom. 'And who is this fine fellow?'

'Tom Marlowe,' said Tom a little nervously. 'Of the Lamb and Lion printing house.'

'And what is a respectable lad like you doing keeping company with one of London's most notorious divers?' Tom turned to Will, who cocked his head and shrugged. 'I see that young Piggot has failed to mention his pickpocketing skills. Tut, tut, Will. Don't be shy, now.'

'Tom, I—' began Will, but Hitchin hit him hard across the side of the head with the back of his hand. Will staggered two steps back, shaking his head, but made no protest.

'Now then,' said Hitchin, pushing Tom gently

to one side. 'If I could just ask you to stand back, Master Marlowe, we shall see what our filthy little friend has in his pockets.' He slowly put on a pair of calfskin gloves and stepped over to Will, smiling. Suddenly he grabbed the boy by the throat with one hand and began patting his clothes with the other. 'Now, what have we here?' he said, and pulled out a silver pocket watch and chain. He squinted at it, reading an inscription on the back: '"For my son, Tom". Well, that's strange, is it not? Your name is Will—'

'The watch is mine,' said Tom.

'Well, that explains it,' said Hitchin.

'I've never seen that watch in my life!' exclaimed Will.

Hitchin hit him again. Harder this time. 'Tell it to someone that cares,' he growled. 'Tell it to the hangman, for all I care!'

'I gave him the watch,' said Tom suddenly.

Hitchin and Will looked equally surprised. 'You did what?' said Hitchin.

'I gave him the watch,' said Tom. 'He saved my life just now. There must be people who saw. I gave him my watch as a reward.'

Hitchin walked slowly towards Tom and leaned forward until the tip of his nose was touching the tip of Tom's. 'And you would swear this in a court of law?'

'I would,' said Tom, edging back a little.

Hitchin remained frozen for a few seconds, staring into Tom's eyes as if looking for something hidden there. Then he suddenly stood upright, took off his gloves and smiled. 'Very well, then, Master Marlowe,' he said. 'I will bid you good day.' And with that he walked away, his two men falling into step behind him.

'That was quick thinking, Tom,' said Will with a laugh. 'I thought he was—'

Tom punched Will on the jaw and sent him spinning towards the wall.

'What's this?' said Will, rubbing his jaw. 'Do I look like I enjoy being smacked?'

'You stole my watch, you thief,' said Tom, fists clenched.

'Thief I am,' said Will, 'but I never stole your watch, you muffin. And don't think about giving me another tap or I shall have to black your eye.'

255

'I suppose it just hopped into your pocket on its own, did it?' shouted Tom.

'It didn't have to,' said Will. 'It had Hitchin to give it a leg-up, didn't it?'

'What are you talking about? How could Hitchin—?'

'Think about it,' said Will. 'When Hitchin eased you out the way, that's when he made the dive. He's not bad, neither. I felt him make the drop into my pocket, but then it's bread and butter to me. I've had more practice.' He put a hand to his chest. 'Look, I swear on my mother's grave. I didn't take your watch, Tom.'

'But why?' said Tom, fists still clenched. 'Why would Hitchin try to get you hanged?'

'Because he's a villain, Tom. They call him a thief-taker, but he's a bigger crook than any he brings in. He has half the pickpockets in London on a leash. He gets them to rob such and such a gent and then charges the selfsame toff a finder's fee for returning the goods. He's been trying to get me to work for him for ages. He's just letting me know he can get me dangled any time he likes. But I'm my own man.'

Tom stared at him and then looked away towards the end of the alley. His hands relaxed.

'I swear, Tom,' said Will. 'I never took your watch. I ain't no liar.' Will smiled a crooked smile. 'Well, not at this particular moment anyways.'

Tom laughed. Will held out his hand and Tom shook it.

'Come on,' said Will. 'Let's get out of this stinking alley.'

'I suppose your mother *is* dead?' said Tom, remembering Will's oath.

'As a hangman's heart,' replied Will.

'Mine too,' said Tom.

Will stopped and slapped Tom in the chest with the back of his hand. 'Then ain't we like brothers in a way?'

'Yes,' said Tom. 'I suppose we are.'

And so, in a way, they had been since that day.

They were an odd couple, but well matched in many ways. Each had a ready wit and a quick temper and both, as young boys, had lost their mothers, which left them with a sadness and an unspoken yearning for something more than they had.

Physically they were very different, though, with Tom black-haired and stocky, and Will blond and skinny as a whippet. Will's clothes were shabby and often much too big for him, emphasizing his slight frame. And he was always in need of a wash that never seemed to come.

Tom talked about his father and the printing shop and Dr Harker. Will loved to hear of the doctor's travels, for just like Tom he had yet to travel five miles from the house in which he was born. For his part Will gave a watered-down account of his life as a member of London's army of pickpockets and petty thieves.

'As it happens,' said Will, suddenly remembering their earlier conversation, 'I don't need your poxy watch, Tom, for I have a rather splendid one of my own. Now let me see – what *is* the time?' With a theatrical flourish, he produced a beautiful gold watch and chain – the very same watch the Cheapside wig-maker had searched for in vain earlier that day.

'Will! For God's sake! Put it away!'

'All right, calm down, Tom,' Will replied, hiding the watch inside his coat. 'Don't have a seizure! There's no one to see us in this fog. Don't get so flustered.'

'*Don't get so flustered?* You could swing for that – and me along with you for not speaking up!'

'No one's going to swing, Tom, though it's good to hear you won't be peaching on me . . .'

'It's not funny, Will. You'll be picking the hangman's pocket one day.'

'Well, you're in a cheery mood today,' said Will, a little crossly. 'You know what I am – what I does. Don't come the parson with me, Tom.'

They both looked down at the ground in front of them and waited for the other to speak. As usual in these situations, it was Will who broke the silence.

'Well, as it happens, Master Marlowe, I happen to have gone and got meself a job.'

'*You?*' gasped Tom.

'Yes, me, you cheeky rogue,' said Will, sounding a little hurt.

'Sorry, Will. That's great news, really it is. I was just a little, well, *surprised*, is all.'

'Yeah, well. I got feelings too, Tom. Lots of 'em.'

'I know, Will, honest I do. Tell me about it. What *is* the work exactly?'

'Well,' said Will, puffing himself up a little, 'I happen to be in the employ of a certain gent I know who has paid me to perform certain very delicate duties.'

'Hmm,' said Tom, raising an eyebrow. 'It is *honest* work, isn't it, Will?'

Will grinned broadly and slapped Tom on the chest with the back of his hand. 'Listen to you. You are such a worrier, Tom. But I can't talk about it, not even to you. Sworn to secrecy and all that.'

'Will . . .'

'I've got to go, Tom. We'll talk later.' And with that Will set off towards the City.

'Will!' called Tom. 'Is it *honest*?'

Will had all but melted into the fog and was a vague and pale sketch when he turned to call back to Tom. 'You could say it's the *opposite* of what I normally do!' Then he turned and, with a little hacking laugh, disappeared like a ghost at dawn.

Tom was just trying to make some kind of sense of what Will had said when a breeze blew in from the Thames and cleared a patch of fog, allowing the houses on the other side of the street to come briefly into view.

Within an instant the fog had closed back in, but in that instant Tom could have sworn he saw someone running along the roof ridge of one of the buildings. He waited to see if the fog would shift again but it seemed set. Tom shook his head. Maybe he was starting to imagine things.

ABOUT THE AUTHOR

Chris Priestley was born in Hull, spent his childhood in Wales and Gibraltar and his teens in Newcastle upon Tyne. He went to art college in Manchester and then lived and worked in London for many years as an illustrator and cartoonist, mainly for newspapers and magazines. He has written a range of books for children, both fiction and non-fiction. He lives in Norfolk with his wife and son.

The Tom Marlowe Adventures are inspired by his own childhood love of historical novels. *Death and the Arrow* was shortlisted for an Edgar Award by the Mystery Writers of America in 2004 and *Redwulf's Curse* was shortlisted for the 2006 Lancashire Fantastic Book Award.

The White Rider

BY CHRIS PRIESTLEY

The man – if man he was – had no face
. . . Where a face should have been there
was only the white bones of a skull!

London, 1716. The alleyways are full of spies
and buzzing with intrigue. The executioner's axe is
wet with the blood of Jacobites who oppose the
reign of King George and flickering lights have
appeared in the sky over the city.

These are strange times, and when Tom Marlowe
and his friend Dr Harker hear stories of the roads
being haunted by a mysterious white rider – a
highwayman who is rumoured to be able to kill
his victims simply by pointing at them – Tom can't
resist the chance to investigate . . .

The second Tom Marlowe Adventure
978 0 552 55474 9

VICTORY

Susan Cooper

Two lives. Two struggles. One battle . . .

Sam Robbins is a farm boy, kidnapped and forced to serve aboard HMS Victory. Lord Nelson's ship at the Battle of Trafalgar in 1805. At first Sam is terrified and seasick, but in the rowdy, dangerous world of the warship, he transforms himself into a sailor and survives a fearsome and bloody battle, the echoes of which reach through the years to touch Molly Jennings. She is a modern-day English girl forced to leave London and live with her new step-family in America, and she too is fighting a battle against loss and loneliness.

This extraordinary time-shifting adventure tells the interwoven stories of Sam and Molly, linked by a mystery. Two lives joined forever by the touch of Nelson, one of the greatest sailors of all time.

978 0 370 32891 1

WOLF GIRL
Theresa Tomlinson

*How far would you go to save your mother
from the hangman's rope?*

Cwen, a poor weaver struggling to make a living
at Whitby Abbey, is accused of possessing a
valuable necklace. If found guilty she could
be hanged, burned or stoned. Wulfram, Cwen's
daughter, desperate to prove her mother's
innocence, encounters lies and treachery
wherever she turns for help.

Set in a turbulent period of Anglo-Saxon
England, this is a story of a resourceful,
dauntless heroine, determined and clever as
a wolf. Defying rank and convention, braving
wind, weather and marauding armies, Wulfran
shows that courage has its own just reward.

978 0 552 55271 4